DANIELLA'S DECISION

DANIELLA'S DECISION

Genevieve Lyons

Chivers Press • G.K. Hall & Co.
Bath, England   Thorndike, Maine USA

F
LYO

LE IC KM RS RS BC BB PW DP BB

This Large Print edition is published by Chivers Press, England, and by G.K. Hall & Co., USA. CA CC

Published in 1999 in the U.K. by arrangement with Severn House Publishers Ltd.

Published in 1999 in the U.S. by arrangement with Chivers Press Ltd.

U.K. Hardcover   ISBN 0-7540-3830-0   (Chivers Large Print)
U.K. Softcover   ISBN 0-7540-3831-9   (Camden Large Print)
U.S. Softcover   ISBN 0-7838-8661-6   (Nightingale Series Edition)

The text of this Large Print edition is unabridged.
Other aspects of the book may vary from the original edition.

Set in 16 pt. New Times Roman.

Printed in Great Britain on acid-free paper.

British Library Cataloguing in Publication Data available

Library of Congress Cataloging-in-Publication Data

Lyons, Genevieve.
    Daniella's decision / Genevieve Lyons.
        p.   cm.
    ISBN 0-7838-8661-6 (lg. print : sc : alk. paper)
    1. Large type books.   I. Title.
    [PR6062.Y627D36   1999]
    823'.914—dc21   99–22229

This book is for my dear friend
Michael Broderick,
and, with my heart,
my daughter Michele.

CHAPTER ONE

Daniel Weston sat in the pink marble foyer of the hotel in Rome, immobile, as if turned to stone. All was busy around her, people coming and going, bells ringing, luggage being transported in and out. Someone shouted, *'Pronto!'* and a small bell-boy hurried past her carrying a square white cardboard box with the name *'de Valliere'* on it in Italian print. At Reception an American was demanding a larger room with a shower and the tight-faced receptionist was muttering something about Rome being built before showers were invented, to which the American cryptically replied that Romans had invented the shower. Ever hear of the baths? he asked him. Somewhere in the distance a woman laughed.

Daniella sat there amid the tumult, hardly seeming to breathe.

She looked incongruous, inappropriately dressed for Rome, and although it was crisply cool in the hotel foyer with the air-conditioning on full blast it was hot and humid outside. Consequently she looked extremely odd in her tweed jacket, grey flannel trousers and cream cashmere sweater while all about her the crowd clothed in airy cottons, linens and silks swirled around her stillness as if she were the eye of a storm. Which, in a way she

1

was. But it was her own storm, an interior storm.

She was wearing what she'd had on when she'd left her home in West Kensington that morning.

She'd been sitting stone-still there too, exactly as she was now in the foyer in Rome, in the armchair in the ultra-neat living-room when Rupert, her husband, had come storming in complaining, accusing, abusing. She had not expected him. At that time of the day he was usually at work. However, he'd forgotten some important papers and, to his annoyance, had had to return to the house to get them. As usual he was blaming her for his forgetfulness.

'You should have reminded me,' he'd thrown at her and proceeded to badger her, accusing her of laziness, droning on and on with the familiar diatribe. Did she *always* sit there doing nothing at that time of the morning when the rest of the world was *active*, except in god-damn Australia? Did she think she was god-damned royalty? More like a zombie, for Christ's sake, and the house a mess and there was so much to be done. Did she expect Dora (the cleaning lady) to do everything? Surely she was capable of *lifting* a duster or polishing silver or doing whatever it was housewives were supposed to do? Some god-damned chore? She was not physically disadvantaged, was she? he'd ask in a reasonable tone but biting off his words like he

2

was tearing off sticky tape. Couldn't she arrange some flowers like other women, or talk to her friends on the telephone? Oh but no! slapping his hand theatrically to his forehead, no! he exclaimed sadly, he forgot. Daniella had no friends. Daniella couldn't keep friends.

And on and on and on he went in that unbearable monotone, sharp as a razor, his voice splitting her head.

He'd only started, he hadn't really got fully into his stride when she had interrupted the flow by standing up and simply walking out. Something she had never done in all the years of their marriage. She'd left the room purposefully and gone into the hall.

Her tweed jacket was hanging on the hall-stand, her handbag dangling by the long strap from the knob of the drawer where they kept keys, stamps, scarves and odd bits and pieces. In that drawer too they stored their passports. Not that they had ever used them. Except for her honeymoon. She had been hardly aware of what she was doing as she had calmly removed hers and put it in her bag and left the house, slamming the door behind her, hearing him yell, 'Where the hell do you think you're going? Come back here at once!'

But she had ignored his orders for the first time in their marriage and continued walking away, her back rigid.

She had almost reached the end of the road

when she turned, unable to resist a backward glance, and there he was at the window, staring after her, his mouth open, aghast. He'd be stunned, she knew that, unable to grasp—any more than she did herself—how she could have done this after all these years. Eight to be exact. Eight years of abuse.

She had walked to the bottom of Lansdowne Road to Holland Park tube station. She took the central line to Holborn and there changed onto the Piccadilly line to Heathrow, all the time feeling like the zombie her husband had accused her of being.

She had stared at the other travellers on her journey to the airport, speculating on their lives, envying their apparent indifference to the rest of humanity. She felt the wonderful detachment that they appeared to possess and was grateful for the suspension of her emotions, but acknowledged to herself, fatalistically, that this calm probably would not last, that she'd eventually have to pay a heavy price for her impulsive action.

She had asked the girl at the British Airways desk to try to fit her onto a plane, any plane, to Rome. The pretty young woman in the uniform was, at first, dubious, but eventually found her a seat on a flight leaving at lunch time. The woman seemed a touch surprised that she had no luggage to check in, but her expression said she'd been trained never to show surprise at the idiosyncrasies of

4

customers.

Daniella went through passport control and settled herself in the departure lounge to wait.

She had remained in a state of near somnambulism, tranquil and unworried. She'd chosen Rome almost as a reflex action. Ariana, her sister, lived there and although Rupert had rarely allowed her to travel alone he had, on occasion, permitted her to visit Ariana.

Ariana had married the son of an Italian business associate of Daniella's and Ariana's father, gone with him to Rome and made her life there.

But Daniella did not want to see Ariana. Her sister was not in the least sympathetic. She said Daniella exasperated her. Ariana had, over the years, when she saw her sister or talked to her on the phone, deplored Daniella's lifestyle, had no time for Rupert and told her sister over and over that his treatment of her appalled her. She criticised Daniella's clothes, saying they were dull and boring and revealed Dani's dismal servitude, for Daniella had let slip that Rupert dictated which outfits she could buy and wear, and she always did as he instructed. It was easier that way.

'You let him walk all over you,' Ariana would lecture her sister. 'He treats you like dirt. How *can* you, Dani?'

How to explain? That he'd make her pay in subtle and unpleasant ways, making her life unbearable. That it was a habit and habit is hard to break. That familiar feeling of being trapped in amber, quite incapable of action, swamped her. And there were all those questions that insinuated themselves between her and flight from her husband. Like, how would she survive without him? Where would she go? What would she do? She'd never been employed, never worked, so how could she get a job when highly qualified people around her were looking for work and not finding it? All very well for Ariana to talk, accuse her of being negative. These were hard facts and anyhow, what no one understood was that she had absolutely no faith in herself. Any confidence she had had been crushed under her husband's heel.

A million questions, unanswerable, sang their song endlessly in her head and she could find no answers and part of her did not even want to. The action would take far more energy than she had, as most of it she used just to survive her daily life with him.

Daniella smiled sadly to herself. Well, something had finally snapped. She'd done it now, though she still had no answers. Here she was sitting in the foyer of a hotel in Rome, quite alone. No one knew where she was, and she hadn't a clue what she would do next.

She supposed Ariana must have been in her mind when she bought the ticket but now that she was here the last person she wanted to face was her sister. Ariana would be triumphant, would say 'I told you so' loudly and vociferously. She would, quite frankly, want to celebrate the break-up of Dani's marriage and Daniella did not feel like celebrating. She felt as if someone had died. Died mercifully, true; but died nevertheless.

Ariana would be the first person Rupert would get in touch with. He'd hate having to contact her. They disliked each other intensely but maintained a civilised if frigid politeness whenever they were thrown into each other's company, which was seldom.

Unless Dani contacted her sister, Ariana would have to say she'd not heard from or seen Daniella for months. The last time they'd spoken Ariana had told her she'd absolutely no sympathy whatsoever for her sister; not any more. She told Dani that the solution to all her problems was in her own hands. 'I'm tired telling you, Dani. Leave the bloody man,' was what she'd said and cut the connection.

Ariana had no idea how difficult that was. So easy to say, almost impossible to do. After eight years, during which she'd been consistently brow-beaten, ridiculed, humiliated, it seemed an impossibility, a more overwhelming challenge than climbing Snowden, or sailing around the world single-handed.

She had believed Rupert, believed all the things he accused her of: laziness, stupidity,

7

muddleheadedness, clumsiness. Why would he say these things if they were not true? She had failed as a wife—the only thing she was qualified for and thought she might do well. It had sapped her confidence to discover she had not been a success, and when she looked in the mirror and saw herself she could only agree with her husband. She was completely and utterly useless.

Ariana was the only one who felt she should leave Rupert. Ariana saw through people. The Westons appeared on the surface an ideal couple. He a successful lawyer, whose reputation as a prosecutor was formidable. He had money; not in the millionaire league though headed there. He had enough to ensure an extremely comfortable lifestyle. And she, a contented wife with the lovely old house on Lansdowne Road to look after. Few knew what went on behind closed doors.

Well, she'd actually left. Daniella sat bemused in the foyer and sometimes people stared. She looked cold on this warm day in her tweed jacket and flannels, so still, so very still.

She wanted to tell Ariana and share what she knew would be her sister's joy at her escape, but she did not want to tell her just yet. It was too soon.

She knew there would be pain, but for the moment there was a great stillness inside her that she did not want disturbed. The

8

realisation of what she had done and the consequences to be faced would come later. She felt so numb, anaesthetised, as if she'd had a couple of drinks or a librium: all smoothed out.

Actually she'd not had anything mind-altering to calm her. She'd refused alcohol on the plane, out of habit.

She liked the feeling of numbness as she sat, immobile, her long bag-strap over one wrist and lying curled, supine on the marble floor beside her chair, like a snake ready to wrap itself violently around a passing ankle.

She sat for a long time in the hotel foyer. People came in and out. The receptionist glanced at her speculatively once or twice. He had his doubts. She'd checked in, but had no luggage.

Her reverie was unexpectedly interrupted by a sharp tug on the strap around her wrist. Someone lurched against her chair and she heard the sound of a crash as the table beside her was knocked over and a man clutched at her jacket sleeve as he fell at her feet. As she opened her mouth to protest, at what she did not know, she saw he'd caught his foot in the strap of her handbag and that it had tightened around his ankle as he'd hurried past her and eventually and inevitably tripped him up.

''Scuse ... Signorina ...' he stammered as he tried to extricate himself from the entanglement and struggled to rise.

A bell-boy rushed to his aid and an elderly couple stood staring down at him as his shoes slipped and slithered on the marble floor.

Daniella jumped to her feet and tried to help but only made matters worse. Clumsy with embarrassment, she pulled at the long strap, tightening its hold on his ankle as he went over again and his leg shot up in the air.

'Oh, I'm so sorry,' she repeated again and again. 'I'm so very sorry.' The man shook his head and waved them all away irritably. '*Prego*,' he cried. 'Look, let me do it. *Pianissimo*!' He untangled the strap and stood, brushing himself down though there was nothing to brush off his elegant suit, the marble floor being spotlessly clean.

'Now,' he said calmly. 'It's all right,' and he looked at her and smiled. 'I wish to apologise. I did not look where I was going and so became, er, entangled in your purse.'

He was much taller than she, dark hair and eyes, clear olive skin and a wide generous mouth. He had an engaging grin and there was a twinkle in his eye as he looked down at her.

'No, no, no. I'm the one who is sorry,' she cried, looking back at him with worried intensity.

He raised his eyes to heaven and spread his hands. 'Why do the English always say that? Sorry, sorry, sorry? You have already apologised. It is all right.' He smiled. 'You are English, are you not?' She nodded. 'Well, then, think nothing of it. You have not killed me, or disabled me.' He gave a little bow. 'Allow me to introduce myself. My name is Marcello Vestori and I apologise, but only once.'

'Please, it was me. My bag. I was to blame . . .' she stammered.

He gave her a dazzling smile. 'Well, since you are so keen, it is all your fault and I accept your apology. Now, why don't you come to the bar with me and have a drink? We both need one, I think?'

Used to being told what to do she obediently took the hand he proffered, rose and followed him.

The bar was dim, almost dark, and smelled mustily of stale cigarette smoke, faintly of beer and wine and air-freshener. The bartender was reading *La Repubblica* but glanced up when they came in.

'What would you like to drink?' Marcello asked her. 'I think you need a cognac.'

'All right.' She never drank brandy but was in no state to argue.

They sat in the curve of a banquette, close together, sipping their drinks. Daniella was tense with embarrassment and the kind of excitement she'd felt on the last day of school.

'You've not introduced yourself,' he said, looking at her with sympathetic eyes.

She told him her name, shook hands with him formally and sipped her drink, looking anywhere in the room except at him.

11

'You are unhappy, Daniella,' he said, a statement rather than a question.

She shook her head vehemently, all her English blood rising in protest at the suggestion that she pitied herself.

'No, no,' she protested, then thinking about Rupert and the facts of the position she was in, she shook her head again. 'Oh, I don't know. I don't know.' Her words tripped to a stop and she bit her lip and whispered again, 'I don't know.'

'I do,' he said softly. 'Look at me,' he told her and obediently she glanced up. His eyes were kind, sympathetic and she felt tears spring to hers at the concern she saw there.

'Tell me about it,' he urged and took her hand across the table. 'After all, we are strangers. What is it?'

She found herself confiding in him, spilling out all the hurt and anger so long imprisoned inside her. At first falteringly, then fluently, she opened her heart and took him into her confidence. He was a stranger, as he had said, and she would never see him again. There was something liberating about dumping all her troubles in his lap. The situation was unhampered by the rules of loyalty and discretion. It was such a relief to unburden herself without consideration of his opinion; whether he would be critical or not did not matter.

She talked of meeting Rupert and falling in

love with him, her hopes and dreams of a life together. She told him how those hopes and dreams had been trampled to death.

'My family were so opposed to the match,' she said. 'They've all been proved right. That's why I don't want to tell them about it.'

She quoted some of the hurtful remarks, the humiliating positions the man she loved had put her in. She confided these things with guileless eyes, half-believing that he would confirm their cruel authenticity, and he returned her open look with a tender compassion.

And the light faded outside and the day slipped into evening and still she talked, and he listened patiently. Bending slightly towards her he listened to her outpouring with an almost professional dedication.

CHAPTER TWO

Daniella and Ariana Panetti were the lovely daughters of an Italian father and an English mother.

Vincente Panetti had opened his restaurant in Greek Street in the Seventies.

It was only in the Fifties that people, ordinary people as apart from the wealthy, began to travel after the war. But it was expensive. In that great rush of adrenalin that was the Sixties it became much cheaper; Thomas Cook introduced the package tour and millions of people became world tourists. Everyone and his wife managed to afford to get away, mainly to Spain. By the Seventies, the demand for Italian, French and Spanish cuisine offered an unbeatable opportunity for cooks, chefs and restaurateurs from those countries to exploit their talent and make a lot of money. The bar café, the bistro, the trattoria, the brasserie and the pizzeria came to England. Cappuccino and espresso, pizza and pasta all became available and familiar.

Of course, there had always been eating houses and foreign restaurants, especially in Soho, but these were mainly for immigrant communities and for visitors sampling strange fare, exotic cuisine. But now everyone, it seemed, was demanding the food they had relished on holidays. They were out and about more too, popping into boutiques, listening to new music, experiencing the new freedoms and dining out on their new 'never had it so good' wealth. Once the preserve of the well-to-do, now such a lifestyle became available to all.

And Vincente Panetti capitalised on that demand and opened Panetti's, which soon became very popular and successful.

At first he had known no one in London, but he quickly made friends, for he was a congenial man. It was the one thing that he found impossible with his son-in-law: Rupert's

14

pronouncements and the impossibility of debate with him.

His best friend, Michaelangelo Maggiore, a wine importer, became like a brother to him. They also became business associates.

Vincente was very happily married. He had advertised for staff and the first applicant for the job of waitress was a beautiful English girl called Rosemary Morris. She had blonde hair, camellia skin and dimples, and she had bowled him over. He had fallen instantly in love with her and she had given up all ambitions to finish her psychology course at London University. She became his wife, business partner and loving companion.

They had two lovely daughters, the eldest, Ariana, pleasing her father no end by marrying Carlo Maggiore, the son of his dear friend Michaelangelo.

The Maggiores had vineyards in Italy, wine outlets in all the European countries, including England. It was, Vincente often said, a perfect marriage, both parties gaining much and losing nothing. Carlo and Ariana were very much in love and they, in their turn, had presented Vincente and Rosemary with two beautiful granddaughters.

Much the same sort of liaison was expected for Daniella. Her father gave a big feast every Monday when the restaurant was closed and invited all his friends, his friends' sons, Carlo's friends, Ariana's friends, the relatives from all over Italy to a sumptuous dinner and celebration. The get-together was a joyous opportunity for sharing marvellous food, drinking good wine, song and laughter and meeting one's own kind.

But Daniella, who had always been shy, had chosen Rupert Weston, someone she had not met in the convivial evenings at Panetti's. An outsider, a cold English gentleman who did not fit easily into the ebullient Italian clan. He was a lawyer she met at Marylebone Magistrate's Court, where she had gone to pick up some papers about her father's wine licence which had to be renewed.

None of the Panettis liked Rupert but Daniella stuck, obstinately, in the face of (and perhaps *because* of) fierce opposition, to her guns. The more obstacles they threw in her path, the harder she fought for Rupert.

She was to suffer untold pain because of her persistence, for she could not admit that they had been right all the time and she had made a terrible mistake.

They had told her over and over again that Rupert was cold. 'A cold fish,' her father said. Rosemary said he'd not be kind to her daughter. 'I know. I can see it in his eyes,' she told Daniella. 'He's got a cruel streak.'

'Unfeeling,' her father said. 'Unfeeling.'

'Oh Dani, he'll not be good to you, my lamb,' her mother implored.

'We love you, *cara mia*,' her father said.

16

'Believe me, he is wrong for you.'

'A man like that, uptight, he'll not make a good lover,' Carlo had said. And they had all been right, only she had been too pig-headed to listen and later would not, could not, admit her stupidity.

Besides, she believed in her heart that no one else would want her. Ariana was the beautiful, confident one and she, Daniella, was lucky to have anyone at all favour her, let alone a bright, handsome lawyer like Rupert. If she turned him down, left him, she'd never find anyone else.

Her disillusionment had started on the honeymoon. Her father had given her a wonderful reception at the restaurant and the present of a honeymoon, all expenses paid, in Positano. It was there that Daniella began to find out what her husband was really like.

Vincente was heartbroken that the ceremony was not a church wedding. 'A marriage not consecrated, how can it work?' he confided his doubts to Rosemary when Daniella told him Rupert insisted on a Registry Office ceremony. Rosemary said she knew the alliance was doomed to failure when she saw how the Westons—Rupert's mother and father, and Rupert himself—treated their food. Vincente had laid on a wonderful meal but Henry Weston, Rupert's father, with his mother, Gladys taking his lead, picked at the meal, suspicious of everything, obviously unused to the exotic tastes. They toyed with the roast peppers, examined the mussels as if they might jump up and bite them, grimaced at the taste of garlic bread. Yet they spoke with grand accents and Henry Weston had been, until his retirement, a respected solicitor.

'Garlic is so *foreign*,' he had told Rosemary, shuddering delicately. 'We English don't like it.'

'I do,' Rosemary had replied succinctly.

'You're English, how can you eat it?' he asked and Rosemary chuckled and said nothing, but in her heart she pitied her daughter and felt yet another surge of apprehension for her future happiness. How could anyone seriously live a full and happy life while disliking Italian food and garlic?

Henry Weston was a small, dapper man. He had the habit of making caustic and detrimental remarks about people not quite out of their hearing and in a bantering tone that was meant to take the sting out of the comment, but did not. Few people had the quickness of recovery from the barb he'd so accurately shot to think of a quick retort, but Daniella's father, who loathed Henry Weston, managed.

'I wonder which side he was on in the war,' Henry had muttered, to which the Italian had instantly replied, 'Unlike you, Henry, I wasn't born then.' Since then the two fathers had been at daggers drawn. The biggest difference between the two men and the characteristic that most defined them was that Henry Weston, in his own estimation, was always right. And Papa Panetti thought that he was mostly wrong. He'd shrug in what Henry called 'a foreign gesture' and say, 'But, I'ma not sure, I'm probably wrong,' laugh and get on with whatever he was doing at the time.

Rupert had had too much to drink at the wedding reception and, although he was not actually drunk on the plane and seemed in possession of all his faculties, he was curiously remote on the drive from Sorrento. She had tentatively touched his hand in the car but he had brushed it away. On the journey along that glorious and fragrant coastline, the sea shimmering in the twilight, she had snuggled up to her new husband, sure now that they could be lovers, but Rupert yet again pulled away from her, then, nodding meaningfully at the driver, very firmly distanced himself from her.

She had thought it was shyness, English reticence, but later, in their cool jasmine-scented bedroom he had not been able to make love to her.

She was a virgin when they married. Her mother had urged Daniella, when all other persuasions failed, to find out what Rupert was like in bed. 'Sex is very important in marriage,' she had told her daughter, clutching at straws. But Daniella had not listened.

19

Rupert would not go to bed with her before their marriage. He seemed shocked by her suggestion that she move in with him and declared that his wife should be a virgin on their wedding day.

'You've never been with anyone else, have you, Daniella?' he'd asked anxiously.

'No. Never,' she'd reassured him. Her father had seen to that. His daughters, until Rupert, had been escorted exclusively by the impeccable company of his friends' sons and they, of course, respecting him and knowing what would happen to them if they dared to take liberties, could be trusted implicitly.

'Oh, that's all right then,' Rupert had said. 'Only I couldn't marry you if you had.'

She should have known then, but, blinded by love, gratitude and hope, the need to prove to her family that she was right and they were wrong, she continued relentlessly in her determination to marry Rupert Weston.

He blamed her the morning after their wedding night. He had fumbled and panted and messed about the night before but to no avail and now he blamed her for his inadequacy. At their first breakfast together he looked at her with cold eyes and said, 'Well, you were a great help last night.'

She'd stared at him, puzzled. 'How do you mean?'

'Oh, for God's sake, Daniella, a man needs a *little* stimulation. Like a dead fish you were, utterly useless.'

She stared at him dumbfounded.

'Why did you behave like that?' he asked.

'What do you mean?' She was bewildered. 'What on earth do you mean, Rupert?'

'Useless. You were useless.'

'I've no experience, Rupert,' she cried apologetically. 'Remember, you wanted so much for me to be a virgin. I don't know what you want.'

'A good wife would,' he told her bitterly.

'I don't understand.' She was near to tears, the piece of toast she was eating stuck in her throat and she felt sick.

'A man needs a wife to encourage him, to . . .' he floundered to a halt. 'You didn't.'

'That's not true, Rupert,' she protested loudly, stung by his accusations.

He glanced around the restaurant, his face flushed. 'Shush! Drawing attention to yourself!'

'I tried, Rupert,' she whispered. 'I tried.'

He leaned towards her. 'You were about as appetising last night as yesterday's dog's dinner.'

Tears stung her eyes and she stared at him uncomprehendingly.

'Now you're going to cry,' he hissed. 'Good God! Why do women always resort to tears when they're in the wrong? That's what my father always says.'

'Oh! Your father?' She thought of the cold

face, the neat moustache and the snide eyes of Henry Weston.

'What do you mean?' he asked suspiciously.

'It's just that you're always quoting your father, Rupert.'

'He knows what he's talking about,' Rupert said sulkily, then angrily, 'Don't you ever criticise my father, you hear me?'

'Oh Rupert, I wouldn't. It's just that no one, your father included, is *always* right.'

'You silly cow! You bitch!'

She had risen but he'd gripped her arm in a steely hold. 'Never, *never* walk out on me! Do you hear? Never do that. Now sit down!'

She'd struggled. A waiter came by and Rupert had quickly let her go. The instant he'd released her, and in spite of his warning glance and his order—for in those days she had not yet learned the penalty for disobedience—she'd fled to the bedroom and thrown herself on the bed. She'd cried herself to sleep.

Rupert had not returned all that day. She stayed in their room, the lovely master bedroom of the hotel, with its view of the sea and the islands. It was meant for honeymoon couples, for billing and cooing, for romance and passion. The balcony looked out over the cobalt-blue sea and the azure sky, but she was all alone, frightened and sick.

She had lunch alone in the restaurant, red-eyed behind dark glasses, unable to ignore the pity in the waiters' eyes. Signor Calione, the

22

proprietor, her father's good friend, tried to talk to her but she shied away from him and returned to their room to lie on the bed and wait.

At last, when it was nearly dark, he had burst into the room. She raised her tear-stained face from the pillow. Rupert stared down at her icily.

'You look disgusting,' he said. 'Now get up and pack.'

'What?' Confused, she gazed at him, hiccuping.

'Pack. We're going back to London.'

'But this is our honeymoon.'

'No. It's a holiday paid for by your father in *his* bloody country among *his* bloody friends. And I'm telling you now, I'd rather we, *neither* of us, accepted *anything* at all from him ever again. Do you hear?'

'But Rupert, he's my papa . . .'

'Shut up! As for *honeymoon*,' his voice dripped scorn, 'some honeymoon! An unwilling bride about as attractive as . . .'

'I'm *not* unwilling . . .'

'I said shut up. Now pack, dammit, pack.'

They'd returned to London and she'd tried to settle down, be a good wife, be what he wanted, do what he expected of her.

They'd gone back to their first home, in those days a flat in Lancaster Gate.

Rupert had changed. Taking her in his arms on their return he'd made heated love to her.

23

It was not very satisfactory for her, it was a quick coupling, but she was so relieved at his obvious excitement and ultimate fulfilment that she believed everything would be all right. She'd decided that it was Italy, the wedding, the travel; she knew he hated travel. He'd been uncomfortable there. Yes, that was it. Wedding nerves and a foreign country drove him to do and say things he did not mean. It was going to be all right.

Everything went well then for about a month. She was the dutiful housewife, cooking, meal on the table when he returned from work, making love before sleep. Fast and furiously to be sure, but then, she supposed that was normal. But he came home one day in a bad mood and started criticising her. The meal she'd cooked he said was disgusting and he'd emptied it into the rubbish bin. Bewildered, she'd tried to placate him but it seemed his fury had to run its course.

After every outburst he'd admonish her, as if she was a child. 'Why do you do this to me?' he'd ask plaintively and she eventually came to believe it was indeed all her fault. She drove him into a bad place and he had to fight his way out and forgive her. Then he'd make love to her and everything would be all right for a while.

She became obsessed with keeping him content, placating him. She learned quickly how to please her husband, what he liked to eat, how he liked the house, how he liked her to be in bed and Rupert responded by being, on the whole, reasonably happy with her. But every so often, no matter how she tried, he blew up, terrifying her, cowing her.

She tried each time it happened to put it behind her, convince herself that it would never happen again, tell herself it was normal and put a good face on it, but underneath she constantly expected for the next outburst, was bruised and hurt by his cruel remarks, his ridicule and contempt.

She never knew when the abuse would begin. Weeks might pass, weeks during which she waited apprehensively, fearfully dreading the inevitable outburst. She became utterly subservient to him, desperate to avoid that terrible cruelty, to keep the peace at all costs.

He was a very successful lawyer. He employed the same biting and accurately cruel assessment of witnesses as he did on her. Judges often had to temper his malign use of language. But it worked. Ninety-five per cent of the time he got his convictions and defence counsel were in awe of him.

They moved after five years from Lancaster Gate down the road to Holland Park and a delightful house on Lansdowne Road. It seemed to the outside world that they had everything.

It was then that Rupert decided he wanted to start a family.

They had no friends. Rupert blamed her for that. At first they'd had dinner parties but she'd been nervous, not of her guests or of her cooking and presentation—she'd had enough experience in the restaurant to be confident of that—but of her husband. He watched her all the time, as if he were waiting to pounce, as if she had to create a fiasco, so that she found it impossible to put people at their ease. They rather tried to put *her* at her ease and unconsciously sided with her husband. 'Poor dear, she's very nervous!' 'Take it easy, Daniella, you're doing fine!'

Rupert always lost his temper afterwards and eventually decided not to invite his friends as she was, as he put it, a 'total disaster area in company'.

She did not get pregnant and once more he blamed her. So she went to see a gynaecologist who examined her, did tests and informed her that there was nothing wrong with her and the trouble was obviously with her husband.

At first, terrified, she kept quiet about this, until one evening, stung beyond endurance by his taunts, she threw the letter at him. It was a letter from the practice suggesting he pay them a visit, reassuring him that there was nothing to it and lots of men had low sperm counts.

He was furious. He lashed out at her with terrifying ferocity. 'How *dare* you, you little bitch!' he yelled red-faced, his eyes wild.

26

'But the doctor said . . .' she sobbed. 'You only need to get some tests . . . It's nothing . . .'

'Doctor!' he shouted. 'Doctor *Elaine* Best! Feminist bloody doctor. You idiot! Can't you see? They'd do anything, say anything, to have you believe, *everyone* believe, that *everything* is the *man's* fault. It's *always* the man's fault. Well, let me tell you, there's nothing wrong with me. Hear that? Nothing!'

It was then that she began to hate him. The resentment built up inside her like a furnace being stoked and she grew to loathe and despise her husband.

On the rare occasions that they went out together, when asked if they had children Rupert would look at her pityingly. 'No, we've no sprogs,' he'd inform the enquirer lightly. 'My wife can't have children, unfortunately.' Any suggestion of adoption or IVE treatment would be brushed briskly aside, the topic changed.

At home, privately in their bedroom he'd say to her, 'I forgive you, my dear. You can't help it, being barren.'

The terrible old-fashioned word pierced her heart and her hatred grew. She could feel the tide of loathing rise in her but, biting her lip, she remained silent. If she rose to the bait and contradicted him she'd suffer for it. He would not speak to her for days except to make some hurtful, derogatory remark.

She'd confided once, long ago, to Ariana,

27

who in any event had guessed the true situation about her marriage. She had regretted telling her sister ever afterwards. Ariana urged her to leave, was impatient with Daniella's tolerance, her excuses, her hope that Rupert would change. Daniella had to admit to herself that one of the reasons she did not leave Rupert was the fact that her sister, of whom she was a little jealous, would say I told you so.

But Daniella was terrified. *Some* of what Rupert said about her must be true. Ariana was her sister so perhaps she couldn't see what others saw. Daniella's deficiencies. So when Ariana urged her to leave Rupert, Daniella pressed her lips together and refused to take her sister's advice. Where would she go? What would she do? Would anyone ever love her? She did not think so. She was not worthy of love and eventually they'd discover her worthlessness.

Rupert loved her. He told her in every hiatus that he loved her, that he forgave her inadequacies, forgave her being childless. Perhaps she'd never again find anyone so forgiving.

Every so often she'd plan to leave him, plot to escape, but she always bottled out at the last moment. The more Rupert vilified her the more dependent she became on him.

And there were happy times. After every outburst there was the absolution ceremony when he formally forgave her her sins and she could bask in his good graces. For a day, a week, a month even. But the anticipation of the next fracas was always there for her just under the surface. When would she fail him again? When would she drive him crazy? Without him what would she do? She had no identity other than Mrs Rupert Weston. Unqualified, stupid, how could she survive without him? Without him she was quite lost.

So she reasoned until that day when that small attack, those not very cruel words, had proved the last straw and she had stood up and walked out, taken a plane to Rome and did things she'd never done before.

Like talking to a complete stranger about the most intimate details of her private life.

CHAPTER THREE

She talked for a long time. The bar filled up with pre-dinner drinkers, then emptied.

Eventually she stopped. She looked exhausted.

'I'm sorry,' she said, then catching his eye she grinned wanly. He laughed and finished his drink.

'What you need is some food,' he told her purposefully, not commenting at all on what she had said. 'Come on. I'll take you to dinner.

One is always hungry after a long chat.'

'I have nothing to wear.' There was a note of panic in her voice. 'Look at me.'

'It's of no consequence,' he told her. 'I'll take you somewhere discreet. And it is cold now. Evening has come. So you'll need your jacket.' He smiled at her as if she was a child and stood. 'Do you want to freshen up? I'll wait for you in the lobby.'

'But you must have plans . . . I have taken up so much of your time . . .'

'No. I'm here on business. All alone. My plan was to dine alone. I'd be glad of your company.'

He was very gracious and she did not believe him, but she felt light-headed and strange. She thought, why not, left the bar and went to her room.

She was surprised to see, glancing in her mirror, that she looked calm and unruffled and there was nothing in her face to show her inner thoughts. In fact she looked pretty. There was a glow on her cheeks and a sparkle in her eyes. In the impersonal surroundings of the hotel room she suddenly felt much more confident.

This man, this Marcello, obviously liked her. He had not run away as Rupert had told her often enough other men would if they got to know her. Not only had he not run away but he had listened to her all afternoon and *then* asked her to dinner.

She knew, of course, what he wanted. Rupert had explained that that was what men wanted from women. He had told her that men's sexual urges were much stronger than women's, which was why he sometimes pounced on her and had to have sex with her instantly no matter how she felt about it. He said that when men looked admiringly at her it was not because she was pretty or attractive but because of this primitive urge that suddenly seized hold of them. It was lascivious, not loving, he said.

'Men need to procreate,' he told her. 'It is their most deep-seated urge. Not that you've been much help in that direction,' he'd added bitterly.

Sex, for Daniella, had become a terrible submission, a negation of herself, an ordeal to be endured, faked, acted without spontaneity or real passion. Of course she read about what it *should* be like, but orgasms, tenderness, foreplay and fulfilment eluded her and she had often wondered about the sensations she read about, which according to the magazines she should be experiencing nightly.

As she stared at her reflection in the mirror an idea entered her head, took root there and became a decision. She'd let this Marcello Vestori make love to her tonight. No matter that his interest would be carnal, that there would be no love. She'd invite him to her room after dinner and go to bed with him. Find out

31

what someone other than Rupert was like, maybe even have an orgasm!

There was a tray on the small table, an electric kettle, little tubs of milk and cream, sealed. There were tiny packets of Nescafé, teabags on the tray. She'd ask him up after dinner for a coffee. If what Rupert said was true he'd make a pass at her and she'd respond. After all, if that was the reason he'd listened so patiently to her, then asked her out to dinner, why disappoint him?

He was a lovely man. She'd noticed the texture of his skin, smooth and fine, the thick darkness of his hair, silver-sprinkled. She'd not mind in the least kissing him, letting him fondle her. She shivered pleasurably at the thought then put on some lipstick, brushed her hair and hurried back downstairs. At last she'd find out what it was like to have sex with a man other than Rupert.

In the lift she thought briefly of AIDS, then decided Marcello would take care of that. If he was not prepared then the hotel were sure to have supplies. But she pushed the thought away determinedly, not knowing how she would manage the niceties of such a situation.

He was waiting for her in the lobby. He turned as she came out of the lift, smiling at her, and she felt her heart take flight. She blushed at her thoughts and he crooked his arm. She slipped hers into his and they left the hotel.

The restaurant he brought her to was a little outside Rome. He drove a Ferrari fast through the streets of the city and down cypress-lined avenues until they reached a wide gravel driveway and a sign, faded, weather-beaten and almost unreadable, fronting an ancient pink house, shaded by eucalyptus trees. It looked run-down and faintly spooky and for a moment she felt fear. The fear of the unknown, then the fear that he was ashamed of her and had brought her to the Italian equivalent of a greasy spoon.

But inside it was another story. The hall he led her into was lined with old family portraits and an ancient but obviously valuable carpet lay on the floor. It led into an impressive dining room, crowded, discreet, busy. Black-suited waiters rushed about and a wonderful and familiar smell of garlic, herbs and spices permeated the air.

The *maître d'* hurried up and greeted her companion enthusiastically. They spoke in Italian but Daniella understood every word.

'Ah, Signor Vestori, how good to see you again. For two?'

'You are very busy tonight, Domini.'

'Very, but then it always is. But we always have room for you.'

'You must come here often then?' Daniella said as they sat and Domini took her white damask napkin, shook it out and placed it over her lap.

33

'You understand Italian?'

'I told you my father is Italian.'

He shrugged. 'That does not mean . . .'

She said, 'He's a restaurateur.'

He smiled. 'Perhaps then I'll let you order for both of us.'

'Oh no!' she protested. 'No. You know what's best here.'

'Everything here is good,' he said and he was right. They had a wonderful antipasto followed by a small helping of *tagliolini ortolano* with spinach and then succulent lamb in a herb crust with fresh mushrooms, ending with *panna cotta*, fruit and espresso.

Marcello kept the conversation light, talking about Rome and complaining vaguely about exhaust fumes.

'In Florence, where I live, a lot of the streets are too narrow for cars. It is a blessing. And, of course, in Venice . . .' he laughed and shrugged.

'In London too it is a nightmare,' she told him. 'The air is actually dangerously polluted . . .'

But they were not really talking about traffic and pollution. He told her about himself. His family manufactured shoes and he lived in Florence with his mother in the family home but came often to Rome, mainly on business.

'I am nothing more than a salesman,' he said, a trifle bitterly, she thought. 'My brother-in-law and my mother really run things.'

34

'That's wonderful,' Daniella cried, thinking of how her mother helped her father, was his right hand.

'You don't know my mother,' Marcello exclaimed, grimacing. 'Oh, I love her, she is wonderful, but . . .' he sighed, 'I will always be *bambino piccolo* to her and she sends me on errands like a little boy.'

They sat for a long time over coffee and brandy and it was late when they left.

Marcello drove the car less tempestuously on the return journey and she could smell the eucalyptus trees. She felt unreal, as if she was in a dream, drifting above herself, watching this bright-eyed girl, hair flying from her face, with this slim, rangy, tanned stranger. Who was she, that woman? A million miles from home and, it seemed, from her character.

In the lobby of the hotel he seemed as if he was about to take leave of her, murmuring goodnight and turning away as if to go, but she put her hand on his sleeve.

'Come and have a last coffee with me?' she asked. He stared at her, frowning, and for a moment she thought she had shocked him. His look slightly puzzled, he followed her to the lift. Her heart was pounding, nearly suffocating her and her hands were shaking.

They went up in silence.

At the door of her room she fumbled with the keys.

'Here, let me do it for you,' he said, taking

35

them from her. The touch of his fingers scorched her hand like a burn.

Inside the room he stood staring at her, perplexed, and she, to her own amazement, felt something she had never felt before, an eager excitement rising in her, making her throat dry and her knees tremble.

They stood there facing each other, then she moved towards him and touched his jacket with her hands, looking up at him, desire in her eyes. He took her in his arms and kissed her.

It was like nothing she had ever experienced. It was soft as cream, sweet as sugar, deep as the ocean. It seemed to her that she melted, that she defrosted into his embrace, his kisses, himself, a long slow dissolving, and bit by bit all her body, every nerve, every muscle, her blood, bones, her very centre became part of him and they moved together, mounting to a moment so fiercely sweet, so overwhelming, she felt acutely alive for the first time in her life.

'So that's what they all talk about,' she sighed, as she lay back on the bed, reluctantly separating her body from his.

'You mean . . .' He raised himself up on his elbow, looking down at her.

'Yes. It's for the first time,' she told him.

'Oh *Mamma mia*! You poor child.'

'No. No, it was wonderful.' She felt the tears prick the corner of her eyes. 'Wonderful.'

'You poor child,' he repeated and perhaps it was that that changed her mood and sent her into a panic. *Poor child*! How hateful! She was not a child to be pitied. Or was she? And suddenly anxiety hit her like an avalanche, gripped her, nearly overwhelming her as her love had overwhelmed her a moment before. She could hardly breathe, the attack was so intense.

What was she doing? Had she taken leave of her senses? Rupert said she was peculiar, an oddity. He said he never knew what to expect of her, that she was not like other women and here she was proving him right!

She had run away from her comfortable home without a change of clothes, from a husband who said he loved her and she could almost swear had never been unfaithful to her. She had checked into a hotel in Rome, not bothered to phone her sister who lived there. No one knew where she was. Her father and mother would be worried. And on top of all that she had picked up a stranger and gone to bed with him. He had not seduced her. If anything *she* had seduced him. Dear Lord, she must be crazy.

'Please go!' she cried suddenly, sitting bolt upright.

'What?' Startled, he stared at her. 'What?'

'Please go,' she repeated, jumping out of the bed, picking up his trousers, thrusting them roughly at him. 'Please, please go.' The panic rose, threatening to choke her.

She was insane. Rupert was right. What kind of woman was she? Behaving like this. She would hurry back to the airport and return to her husband, to her home. She must truly have been mad.

'What is all this about?' Marcello was asking her. 'What have I done? Have I said something? To upset you?'

'Oh no, just go,' she urged, panic-stricken.

He was pulling on his pants and she could not see his face. She thrust his shirt at him and almost pushed him into the corridor. As she did so a couple were going into the room opposite and the man raised his eyebrows and the woman looked amused. Daniella realised she was naked.

'Goodbye,' she cried out and slammed the door shut. She leaned against it, panting, her mind a tangle. What had possessed her? As if she was not in enough trouble without that, getting involved with a man she did not know.

She crawled into bed, pulling the sheets around her and squeezing her eyes shut. Oh God, let it go away, let it all go away.

She fell asleep and dreamed fitfully of his beautiful body, his tender lovemaking, and all the time Rupert loomed over them. She groaned in her sleep, but at last lost consciousness. It had been a long day.

CHAPTER FOUR

The next morning she phoned Ariana.

'I've left him.'

'I guessed. He phoned me.' Daniella waited for the tirade of 'I told you so!' but it did not come.

'Where are you?'

'Here. Rome. A hotel. The Via Condotti.'

'Stay there. I'll fetch you at once. Oh Dani, I'm so pleased. It must have taken courage.'

Daniella was not feeling pleased or courageous; she was in turmoil. Her body had never felt so languid, so liquid, so relaxed. Never in her whole life had it felt so much a part of the world, the sun, the flowers, nature. She was utterly in tune. Physically, that was. Mentally, it was quite another matter. Her mind was in a whirl.

It would take Ariana some time to drive down from her villa in the hills and Daniella was starving. That was another new thing. She never felt hungry in the morning but today she was ravenous.

She dared not go down to the restaurant for breakfast. Marcello might be there and she knew she could not face him. She picked up the phone and ordered hot croissants, coffee and orange juice. They said they'd send it up right away.

When the knock came to the door she assumed it was her order and she answered it at once. But when she opened the door Marcello was standing there.

She stood in the doorway like a guilty child looking up at him.

'I wanted to know, to ask, what happened?' he said.

'I . . .' she hesitated, not knowing what to answer, puzzled by his hurt expression.

'Why did you treat me like that?' he asked and there was a hint of anger in his voice.

'I behaved badly, I know,' she replied.

'You *used* me,' he told her. 'You used me, then discarded me. Do you have any idea how that felt?'

Startled by his words she looked down, unable to meet his clear eyes. She realised suddenly that she knew exactly how terrible he felt. She had been there many a time and it was horrible. She opened her mouth to apologise, say she had not meant to hurt, and looked up to tell him but he had gone. The bell-boy stood there with a laden silver tray in his hands.

She looked with distaste at the croissants. They looked inviting folded in their snug little white napkin but she had lost her appetite.

There was another knock at the door and she rushed over thinking it might be Marcello again, but it was Ariana.

'Well, Dani, how good to see you,' Ariana

cried sweeping her sister into a large embrace. 'Oh I'm so glad. So glad.'

'When did you speak to him?'

'He phoned last night.' Ariana settled herself in an armchair near the window. 'His voice was an octave above the norm. He tried to pretend there was nothing wrong, Dani, asking for you oh so casually. I said truthfully that I didn't know where you were. That you were not with me.' She opened her bag, took out a packet of cigarettes and lit a Marlboro. Daniella backed away but Ariana did not seem to notice her distaste. She continued, 'I knew you'd finally got the courage to leave. You'd never have gone somewhere and not told him. You'd be too afraid of the consequences. Oh my poor lamb. You've had such a terrible time.' She stood up.

Her sister, Dani thought, not for the first time, was everything she was not. Tall, elegant, not a hair out of place, she was the epitome of fulfilled, successful womanhood. Whereas Daniella was a sort of mongrel combination of Vincente and Rosemary, her hair being brown, her eyes hazel, her build small, elfin-like. Ariana was a carbon copy of her mother, long legs, wide mouth, full lips, natural blond hair and cornflower-blue eyes. She had a doting husband and two beautiful children, ran an art gallery off the Piazza di Spagna and a beautiful home on one of Rome's seven hills.

'You got any luggage?' she asked now and

41

Daniella shook her head.

Ariana laughed. 'Just like you.'

Stung, Daniella asked, 'What do you mean?'

'Only that you are so sweet. If it was me I'd pack all my valuables first. I'm not as nice as you are, pet.' She gave her sister an impulsive hug. 'Off we go,' she smiled. 'Come on. You need some TLC.'

There was no sign of Marcello as they paid the bill and left the hotel. Ariana drove in her little yellow Citroën out through the roar of the Vespas and the heavy morning traffic to the trees and the yellow and green of Rome's hillsides.

The villa, Ariana's and Carlo's home, was big and cool and spacious. From her window Daniella could see the Vatican City shrouded in a misty blue haze. It looked like a film set. All around were dotted lines of cypress and further out the olive groves. She kicked off her shoes and peeled off her socks and padded barefoot across the cool marble floor. She felt freer than ever before, like a child let off school, but guilty too, like a child with a secret.

Ariana lent her some light summer dresses she had bought in Positano. At the mention of that name the memory of her honeymoon came rushing back unpleasantly to Daniella. The dresses were silk, one a light raspberry colour printed with little sprays of yellow flowers, the other with tiny red sprays of rosebuds. They lay on the bed where Ariana

42

draped them looking bright and gay. Seeing her hesitation Ariana told her to keep both.

'They're so pretty, Ariana. But I never wear such colours.'

'Do. It will make you feel better. I can get more like them.'

'In Positano?'

Ariana nodded, then clapped her hand to her mouth. 'Oh God! That's where you went for your honeymoon, isn't it?'

Daniella nodded. 'But it doesn't matter now, Ari,' she lied. 'It doesn't hurt so much any more, is what I mean,' she added truthfully. She was thinking of Marcello, intimate things that made her blush. How long his body was, lean and olive-skinned and infinitely seductive. That hurt. There was an ache inside her she'd never experienced before and she wondered briefly if she'd ever be free of pain. Had she swapped the hurt of Rupert for another, more acute form of suffering?

'There now, pet.' Her sister came over and sat beside her on the bed, taking Daniella's hands between hers. 'It's tough, I know. But you'll recover. We all do. Broken hearts only happen to teenagers and the very old. Not to us though.'

She thinks I'm grieving for Rupert, Daniella realised, and I'll not shed a tear over him. I feel nothing for him, absolutely nothing. No guilt, no pity, no pain.

All she felt was the legacy he had left her

43

with, the loss of confidence, the low self-worth, the self-disgust.

But Marcello. Oh, that was a different story. She felt that she had held something infinitely precious for a little moment and then smashed it.

'You can stay here as long as you like, Dani. Carlo and I will look after you till you get over it all, decide what to do.' She rose. 'Now have a shower and put on one of these dresses. I think the yellow one will suit you best. It's cheerful. We'll have lunch in about an hour. On the terrace,' and she left the room, closing the door softly behind her. It was only then that Daniella realised her sister had not once said 'I told you so'.

CHAPTER FIVE

Rupert Weston lost his case that morning, much to the astonishment of the defence, the judge and the accused.

Bruiser Bestwick, a little weed of a con man despite his name, couldn't believe his luck when he walked from the court a free man, no stain on his character.

'Messed that one up, old boy,' Colin Denver-Garantel remarked good-humouredly as he passed his colleague in the corridor outside. 'Not like you at all.'

44

Rupert grinned sourly and hurried out of the building into the glorious May day.

Where was she? Where in the name of heaven was Daniella?

He crossed the street and went into the Rat and Parrot, automatically ducking his head as he did so to avoid the low beams. He ordered a ploughman's lunch and a pint and sat alone, brooding. Others from the court came in and out, greeting each other, laughing, exchanging ribald jokes or pieces of information with serious faces, slapping each other on the back, buying each other drinks. But no one joined him. They left him alone.

Rupert didn't mind. He'd never cultivated friends. His father had always warned him about the danger of outsiders, the foolishness of trusting people. 'They always *want* something from you, boy. Always on the take. Always let you down. No, the pound in your pocket is worth more than anybody and don't you forget it. *Keep it there*. It will help you more than any friend, believe you me. Buying drinks for people, not a good idea. You get taken for a fool. People think you are a pushover. Find a good woman. Stick with her.'

Rupert's mother was just such a woman. A little bird-like creature who echoed her husband in all things and had no opinions of her own, or at least none that Rupert had ever heard her utter. She scurried about ministering unto her husband, washing, cooking, cleaning.

The Westons were not too happy about their son's marriage to Daniella.

'Italian blood! Foreign!' They were xenophobic. They never left England, spending their holidays in Whitby and Southwold and creating in their son a fear and dislike of foreigners equal to their own.

But, contrary-wise, he had chosen, to their horror, an Italian-London beauty. Because she was half-Italian he felt infinitely superior to her. Unlike his mother and father, who were one hundred per cent English and were quite happy to be insular together, he had put himself in a position of superiority and that gave him a great sense of power.

Sometimes, in the beginning, however, she had seemed not to understand this, so he had tried to teach her.

His father had moulded him in his own image and likeness. Rupert adored him. He was up there, on a pedestal, his every word cherished, laws to the young boy.

However, there had been one day, a day he never forgot. He had come home from school with a painting he'd laboured over. Miss Menzies, the art teacher, said he had real talent. He must have been about six years old. The painting was of trees and she'd said it was very good. 'Show that to your parents, Rupert. Take it home. They'll be ever so proud.'

He'd worked at it painstakingly. The tree had a nest with a bird in it. He had to admit

46

that the bird and the nest did look a little awkward where they were, sort of *balanced* on the edge of a leaf. But the tree and the leaves were perfect. He'd done the leaves so carefully, outlining each meticulously, and there had been *hundreds*. Well, it was a big tree.

His father had glanced at it and Rupert, in an agony of expectation, waited. His father *must* be pleased with him, he'd congratulate him, tell him he was a good boy, that the painting was wonderful. And he stood, chewing his bottom lip, twisting his hands together fiercely, waiting for the verdict.

'Couldn't you have done better than that, sprog?' his father asked and crumpled the painting and threw it in the waste-paper basket.

'You must try harder, sprog. It's amateurish.'

His mother had secretly retrieved the painting and smoothed it out. She'd hung it in his room, round the side of a panel where it couldn't be seen from the door. His father never came further into his room than the doorway.

'Amateur means love,' she'd whispered. 'An amateur does something because they love it.' It was the only time she'd ever been anything but an echo of Henry Weston.

His father had told him, 'Don't trust anybody, young shaver, Miss ... Miss ... the art teacher is lying. That's why she said it was good when obviously it is not. Not up to scratch at all. No, she wants something from you, bet on it.'

He had been right. Next day when she'd asked him where the painting was he said his father had thrown it away. He did not yet know his mother had saved it.

'Why, Rupert? It was so good.'

'My father didn't think so.'

'Oh! Well, tell you what. You do something for me, will you?' and she smiled at him. 'I'll let you put out all the paint pots for me this morning. All right? And you can mix some of the colours for me, there's a good boy.'

Mutinously he had done as she asked. Yes, his father had been right. He always was.

'Marry a woman like your mother, Rupert. Women are like horses. Have to be broken in. Show who's boss and you'll have no trouble. Give them an inch and they'll walk all over you.'

Well, he'd tried with Daniella and had had success, he'd thought, until now. What the hell had happened? Where the hell was she?

It was a mess at home. He was not sure exactly where anything was. She had laid out his shirt and underwear for him while he was in the bathroom each morning, just as his mother did for his father. This morning he'd wanted to wear a pink shirt and he couldn't find it. He'd given it to her last Friday but it

48

wasn't in the drawer where he kept his laundered shirts. Nor could he find socks to match the blue shirt he'd eventually decided on. He'd emptied out the drawer in a temper, leaving the socks spilled out all over the floor. He knew he'd return home to face that mess. No Daniella to tidy up. Where was she? He hated mess. Untidiness made him physically ill.

Then there'd been the coffee. He'd eventually given up trying to manage those infernal machines and for the first time in eight years left home without drinking a cup of hot freshly ground Colombian coffee. His favourite.

He could not work out how the grinder or the cafetière worked. He knew it was simple but he had neither the time nor the patience to prepare it and he'd been all fingers and thumbs. The coffee beans were everywhere and there was burnt toast stuck in the toaster.

It had been ghastly. He'd have to get her back a.s.a.p., teach her a lesson and, as his father was fond of saying, 'lick her into shape'.

'Hello, Rupert. Why so gloomy? Because of the Bruiser Bestwick case? Eh? Sour grapes! Well, I have to say it was your fault. You muffed it badly.'

Selina Wright plonked herself down opposite him without a by-your-leave. He glared at her. She was the sort of woman he despised, and, if the truth were told, was not a little afraid of. Petrified, to be specific.

49

She reminded him of Ariana, his sister-in-law. A confident woman, unafraid, tall and certain of herself, striding the corridors of power as if she had every right to be there. As if the men were not making a huge sacrifice permitting her a niche in their rightful world.

There were differences. Ariana was blonde and Selina had a tangle of wild dark hair, brushed out pre-Raphaelite style around a small mischievous face. She was a formidable advocate—which was no job for a woman—a defence lawyer he'd learned not to underestimate.

'Oh, don't *lower* at me like that Rupert. It doesn't impress me at all. No,' she leaned her elbows on the edge of the table inspecting him, 'I'm interested. Whatever happened to that vitriolic tongue this morning? Lost it, Rupe?' she laughed. He glared at her, wanting to kill her.

'Oh, shut up, Selina and go away. I've got other things on my mind.'

'Well, that explains it. But it's not like you, is it? So what?' She stared at him with avid interest. 'Can't be that bad.'

'Well, it is!'

She laughed in a superior way that infuriated him. 'Nonsense, Rupe. You've got it made. You're a bloody cold fish and I often wonder if you've got any feelings at all.'

'Daniella left me!' he cried angrily, dramatically, unable to keep the disaster to himself a moment longer.

He wanted to startle the bitch, shock her, but she grinned at him, retorting coolly, 'Good for her! Well, well, well, wonders never cease. So little Dani got the courage after all these years.'

He looked at her, genuinely puzzled. 'What do you mean?'

'I'm surprised she lasted this long,' Selina replied tranquilly.

'Why on earth would you say that?'

She shook her head gently. 'You don't understand, Rupert, do you? You really don't.'

'I don't know what you are talking about,' he cried defensively. The conversation was not going the right way at all. She should have been shocked, astonished, full of sympathy for him. It was making him very uncomfortable.

'Everyone in this world is not your enemy, Rupert. You treat people with arrogance, contempt and dislike so that's what you get back. It's also why you win so many cases.' She leaned forward, speaking earnestly. 'You carry on as if everyone is out to screw you. Well, would you believe, Rupert, they are not! Actually, most people are nice. Can you credit that? Especially Daniella. She's a sweetie. Though I've often wanted to shake her.'

'You don't *know* her.'

'Yes, I do. We ate a lot in Panetti's, our family. I like their family,' she frowned, 'and I suppose you are right, I don't know Daniella

51

that well. But I've seen her around with you, on the few occasions you grace us with your company. Compulsory dos. I remember going to their restaurant in Soho with my father and mother and Daniella being a bright little girl, about my own age, with sparkling eyes.' She looked at him intently. 'You put out that sparkle, Rupert. I've seen it. Over the years.'

He rose. 'I don't have to sit here and listen to—'

'Sit down!' she snapped. He obeyed. 'That's better,' she said, then stared at him.

'You want her back?'

He nodded. 'Have you any idea how to achieve that?'

He shook his head. She raised her eyes heavenward.

'Any idea why she left?'

'None,' he said, then thought about all her mistakes. 'Well, I couldn't . . . Women have to learn how to . . . She didn't always do what she . . .'

She let him flounder, watching him closely.

'Well, women like to know who's boss. Otherwise things get out of hand,' he announced firmly.

'Oh, is that so? And who pray told you that?'

'My father.'

'Poor Rupert.' He flushed. 'Have you ever heard of *partnership*?' she asked quietly.

'Doesn't work. Not in marriage.'

52

'Yes, it does. That's where it works best.' He shook his head and she added, 'Think of Daniella's mother and father.'

'But they are Italian. A different kind of people. At least her father is.'

'And what, may I ask, has that got to do with it?'

'They're different to us,' he said stubbornly.

'How?'

'They're not English.'

'Again, what's that got to do with it? You ever read Shakespeare?'

'Course!'

'*Merchant of Venice*?'

'Yes, but what . . .'

' " . . . If you prick us do we not bleed? If you tickle us, do we not laugh? If you poison us do we not die . . ." '

'Oh for Pete's sake . . .'

'All people are the same, Rupert, underneath. No matter what your father has told you. Chinese, Russians, Americans, Africans, yes, and Italians, feel love just as we do, have hopes and dreams just like us, feel fear and despair, anger and joy. We *look* different, but don't be fooled. Inside we all have the same emotions. Identically. Think on it. It is *how* we react to those feelings that differentiates us. And we have honourable and dishonourable people in every race. The baddies and the goodies. And if we dare to trample on the delicate feelings of others we

53

must beware the result.' She rose and finished her drink in one most unlady like gulp, slinging her bag over her shoulder.

'See you around, Rupert,' she said and turned to leave.

'But you said you'd tell me how to get her back.' He stopped her in her tracks.

'You'll have to figure that one out for yourself, Rupe,' she laughed and shook her head. 'You really are a dinosaur, you know. Bye.' And she swept out, leaving him shaken and stirred-up and more confused than he'd ever been in his life before.

His father had made it all so simple for him and here was this girl complicating it, unbelievably muddling him.

He sighed and returned to his speculations. Where was she? Where could she have gone?

There was only one place and that was to her sister. Well then, that was where he would go. Foreign parts or no. He'd only been out of England once in his life on that terrible honeymoon when he'd not been able to perform.

But that had been her fault. No doubt about it. And the bloody country! He'd hated it. People speaking another language, not being able to understand what they said. Driving on the wrong side of the road. Foreign currency. Strange food. Not being *in charge*. But he'd got to get her back.

Not just yet though. Let her stew a while,

find out how much she needed him, realise she was nothing without him. Had nothing. No home. No money. No position. No man to lean on.

Oh, she'd realise soon enough how foolish she'd been. He'd forgive her though. He smiled to himself at his magnanimity. He'd give her a good talking-to first though. Show her who was boss. Bring her home where she belonged. Yes, that's what he would do.

Satisfied, feeling much better, he finished his lunch and left the dim interior of the pub and, crossing the road, returned to the courts. There would be no more failures that day.

CHAPTER SIX

It was not, however, as easy as that. Returning home that evening to the empty house in Lansdowne Road to find it exactly as he'd left it—coffee beans, socks in disarray—depressed Rupert unbearably. Like an adolescent, he felt wave after wave of conflicting emotions swamp him. Her warm welcome, missing the sight of her smiling face, made him shiver with loneliness. No delicious meal waiting for him reminded him how hungry he was. He sat down in his beautifully minimal Colefax-and-Fowler-designed living-room and wrung his hands.

55

There was no appetising smell coming from the kitchen. How could he unwind with no wife to hassle? Thoroughly disgruntled he cast around in his mind for someone to unload his troubles onto and could come up with no one at all.

Except his father. At least at home he'd get a decent meal. He thought for a moment. Thursday. There would be shepherd's pie and apple crumble. There always was on Thursday.

He left the house, got into the Golf, and drove to Finchley.

London looked beautiful but he did not notice the greenery, the pale mauve of the wisteria, the lilac, the splashes of scarlet peonies and rhododendrons, the thick sunburst swatches of laburnum and the delicate white frou-frou of the hawthorn and apple blossom.

His parents' home, a detached small compact house, neat as a painting, set in a small English country garden, brought back to Rupert a feeling of security. Coming home from school, fearful of the progress reports he carried in his satchel, too chicken not to hand over, but aware that they were nearly always good. That he would be, not applauded—his father never applauded—but reassured that he had *not done badly*. And the euphoric sensation of returning from boarding school, later, looking forward to blue days at Southwold. Sea and sand and buckets and spades. His father was hot on buckets and spades.

He parked the car and sat for a while in thought. He was aware that his father would cry triumphantly, 'I told you so', but Rupert felt he could bear that if his father told him how to get Daniella back. He'd know what to do. He always knew what to do, but how could you lick someone into shape when they weren't there? He'd ask and his father would have the answer.

He looked at his watch. It was eight-thirty. Dinner would be over. His father would be reading *The Times* in the front room. He always read the papers until the nine o'clock news on BBC 1. His mother would be in the kitchen cleaning up after supper, washing the dishes. She'd join Henry in the front room for the news. She'd bring her knitting or the mending in and sit in an upright chair nodding at what her husband said, agreeing with his comments. Why couldn't Daniella agree with him like that? He always felt, with her, that it was because she wanted to avoid a row. Mind you, she had been much more biddable in recent years. She had learned and Rupert was grateful that his father's teaching had, in fact, paid off. That was why he felt things would be all right. She *was* capable of learning, only it seemed she'd forgotten the lesson.

It was very reassuring to know exactly what his mother and father would be doing, where they would be. There was a nice warm feeling around Rupert's heart at the thought that they invariably followed an exact routine and he could picture them in his mind at any time of the day or night in their domestic setting, behaving as they had for years, never deviating, always predictable.

He smiled to himself as he crossed the road, hurrying the last few yards to the front door, anxious to get into that familiar scene.

But he was in for a surprise. He had, in the upset, forgotten his front-door key and he had to ring the chime. He shuffled impatiently as he waited for the door to be opened. The chime sang out 'There'll always be an England' but when finally the front door was pulled back he got the shock of his life.

His mother had always been a drab little creature and if pressed to describe her Rupert would have had great difficulty. She was like a busy little sparrow, dun-coloured and self-effacing. The woman at the door wore a bright cerise dress with black polka-dots on it. Her hair was hennaed a dubious red and she wore scarlet lipstick and high stiletto heels.

For a second Rupert thought it was someone else but the woman pulled him into the hall, exclaiming in his mother's voice, 'At last! Oh Rupert, you finally got my message! I've been trying to get you for days!'

'Mother? What is it? Why are you dressed like that?'

She glanced down, giggled unnaturally.

'Oh this! This is just an experiment. Janey was here and . . .' She petered out, glancing up the stairs.

Janey was his aunt, his mother's sister. She was thoroughly disapproved of by Rupert's father and therefore by Rupert. Janey and his mother met in secret, rather like, he often thought, how Daniella and Ariana met. They had a rendezvous the first Wednesday of every month in the tea-rooms on Finchley High Road.

'Auntie Janey *here*?' Rupert was incredulous. When he was young his mother, during the holidays, when they were not at Southwold or Whitby, used to bring him to the tea-rooms and swear him to absolute secrecy. Auntie Janey *in the house* was unheard of.

'Yes, dear.' His mother's eyes, he noticed now, were a bright deep shade of blue. He'd never been aware of their fierce colour before. In fact it surprised him. He'd always thought of them as grey.

His head was in a whirl. He tried to grasp what was happening but could make no sense of it. He felt he'd stepped into a dream where everything familiar had become outlandish, unrecognisable.

'Mother, what's going on?'

'Didn't you get my message?'

'What message? Mother, will you please tell me—'

'I left a message at your office. There was no reply at your home.'

'I haven't *been* to the office for days. I've been at home and in court.'

'Well, I left a message at your office *and* at your home. You must have forgotten to look.'

That was true. He hadn't bothered to check. He'd been too distracted.

'Your father's had a stroke.'

'What?'

'Your father, dear. He's had a stroke. He's upstairs . . .'

'My father? A stroke . . .'

Patiently, 'Yes, dear.'

'Shouldn't he be in hospital?'

'Yes,' she looked defensive. 'Well, he *was*. Yesterday. But they sent him home. Said there was nothing they could do. They're sending an ambulance for him in the morning to take him to Paddington. Apparently they haven't a bed for him around here.' She did not seem too concerned and Rupert felt his irritation rise. He'd come here for comfort and advice only to find a muddle.

'But that's crazy.'

'Well dear, it's the best we can do.'

Looking at her he thought, she's enjoying this. She's actually having fun. A great rage engulfed him, broke over him like a wave, then receded and left him cold.

'So you decided to dress up like a tart while my father lies helpless upstairs . . .'

'Don't you *dare*, Rupert.' Her eyes were snapping and she spoke in a cold, resolute voice he'd never heard before.

They were still standing in the hall and every so often his mother glanced up the stairs but instead of lowering her voice when she did so, she raised it slightly.

'I've *slaved* after that man . . .' she cried loudly.

'My *father* . . .' he insisted, shocked.

'Your father, yes. He's bossed me and bullied me. He's lorded it over me and crushed me under his great ugly feet. And you know what, Rupert?' she was suddenly conversational, 'I'm *glad* he's helpless. I'm free of him at last and I'll dress up as anything I damn well please.'

'Mother!'

'I've tiptoed around him, fed his ego, never expressed an opinion of my own.' She looked at Rupert and he saw that her eyes were getting bluer all the time. 'And he told me all the time that this was love. Well, Rupert, I've information for you. It's not! It's not even a distant relation of love. I loathe the man. Despise him. And I'll live to dance on his grave.'

Rupert stared at this woman, a stranger who was his mother, and as he gawped at her, speechless, a terrible roar shook the house and looking up they saw Henry standing, swaying, at the top of the stairs. How he got there was

61

never explained. Some electrical impulse of nerves or reflexes propelled him to that last expenditure of energy. Who knows?

He wore his pyjamas and he had not shaved or been shaved for days. He looked frail and emaciated and terrible at the same time.

The roar he uttered was cracked and hollow but loud, a horrible noise, and his eyes were wild. He must have dragged himself out of bed and onto the landing and now he stood there leaning on the banisters. He was trying to speak but all that came out of him was this croaking call, like a crow.

'Going to lay down the law, are you?' his mother screeched up at him, her voice vindictive and angry. 'Well, you've done that for the last time.' Then, taking a deep breath she yelled, 'Get back to bed *at once! At once*, do you hear me? At once.'

CHAPTER SEVEN

They sat at the kitchen table as they used to when he was small. He never remembered his father being in the kitchen at all.

He still felt oddly uncomfortable with his mother looking as she did, eyes glittering feverishly, voice confident, made-up and dressed-up uncharacteristically. Looking, as he'd said, like a tart.

'Why did you shout at him like that?' Rupert asked.

'It's about time, Rupert, isn't it? He's shouted at me all these years.'

'No, he didn't,' Rupert contradicted her. 'I never remember him shouting.'

'He didn't have to,' she insisted, slumping, as if all energy had left her. 'Oh, he shouted at me all right, *screamed* at me all these years, Rupert, only silently, so *you* never heard him.'

'Mother, you're upset . . .'

'It's time I became a *person*. That I found out *who* I am.'

'You are Father's wife. My mother,' he told her. She shook her head violently.

'No, no! I'm Gladys. That's who I am. Gladys.' She cocked her head and looked at him sideways. 'I bet you never, ever thought of me as Gladys? Well, that's who I am, Rupert. But I've never been allowed to be who I am.'

'Oh, that's nonsense, Mother. It's psycho-babble. It's the shock, isn't it? You're in shock.' Rupert smiled now he had an explanation for her behaviour. 'You're his wife and my mother.'

'A shadow is what I am. And, my dear, that is not what I should be.'

'Well, I . . . Shock, is what . . .'

'Do you know my favourite colour? Flower? Food? What music I like best? What I think politically? Am I Conservative or Labour?'

'Conservative, of course. Father always said

Labour was for the scum of the earth, drop-outs, vagrants, free-loaders ... He said you were the same as him.'

'Well, I'm not. I voted Lib Dem, so there!' She looked at her son defiantly. 'It was the one thing he couldn't control me about and I lied to him about it. To keep the peace.' She stared at her son, then gently covered his hand with hers. 'You haven't a clue who I am, Rupert, have you? What my likes and dislikes are?' She sighed sadly. 'And to tell you the truth, after all this time I'm not sure I know myself.'

He did not know what to say, what to do. He'd gone upstairs and seen his father, in the double bed in the master bedroom, lying there helpless, his eyes crazy. This room had been his parents' room, shared for all those years, and now every trace of his mother had been eradicated. Not that she'd stamped her personality on the room very distinctively in the first place, but Rupert remembered a box of Coty face powder, orange with little powder-puffs dotted all over it, a bottle of Tweed perfume and sometimes some jewellery on the dressing table.

She'd moved, she told him, into *his* room. The room he'd occupied all his life. She'd moved in as if he'd never been the occupant, eradicating him.

He'd peeped in when she went downstairs to make a cup of tea and seen bright dresses slung carelessly here and there, not very tidily.

64

Obviously Auntie Janey's. Auntie Janey'd always worn bright colours as if, Rupert decided, she was in competition with nature and she was determined to win. He'd often thought, send her to the tropics! Send her to Tahiti, see if she would dominate there!

An emerald-green frock hung on the wardrobe door over his cricket banner, partly concealing it. There was make-up, lipsticks and vile-looking nail varnish on his desk with a bottle of Christian Dior Poison. And an opened Strawberry Blond Hair Colour Semi-Permanent Rinse took pride of place with all the rest of the vanity paraphernalia.

He shuddered. It seemed like a desecration. Whenever he'd returned home the room was always as he left it and now there was hardly a familiar sign of his occupation. He could just glimpse his cricket cap in a corner and a few books with a towel thrown carelessly over them, and everywhere, he thought, vulgarity.

It was Auntie Janey, he was sure, and he shuddered angrily, deciding bitterly that they had lost no time. His poor father, felled by a stroke and at once everything changed. His father did not like change.

Rupert had said as much when he'd come down to the kitchen and she'd replied cynically, 'Oh, Rupert, I've lost far too much time.'

He'd come to tell them about Daniella, listen to them commiserate with him about his

65

wayward wife. They would, he'd anticipated, all agree that Italians were unpredictable and unreasonable and most of all *not English*. They'd be of one mind, his father, his mother and himself. And instead of this comforting unity of thought and hopefully advice on how to put it right he'd been met by a disabled father screeching incomprehensively and a mother who was behaving like a Nazi commandant dressed like Mata Hari instead of the sweet, gentle woman he'd known all his life.

'I don't understand anything any more,' he said hopelessly. She looked at him brightly with those new eyes.

'Well, Rupert, that's a very good place to start,' she said enigmatically. 'A very good place.'

She'd given his hand a squeeze and he'd realised suddenly that he'd get no help from her. None at all.

CHAPTER EIGHT

Waking up free from fear reminded Daniella of her childhood, coming-to in her little bed over the restaurant in Soho. The smells of food, the warm knowledge that her parents were downstairs, up and about, doing their chores energetically, and she was cocooned in a blanket of love and concern. The kind of concern that sharpened the edges of her mother's voice and made her father frown. Love.

Since her marriage to Rupert she had not had any such awakenings. Fear clutched her before she even opened her eyes and grim voices whispered in her ears.

Today, however was different. Since she had come to her sister's house that old relaxed serenity had returned and she turned in her bed and smiled to herself at the absence of tension, the blessed *absence*.

Later, on the terrace, the children clung to her knees. They looked to Daniella like dolls in their pretty dresses. They had masses of soft curly hair that smelled of baby shampoo, and big expectant eyes.

Carla and Paola.

They reminded Daniella of herself and Ariana when they were young. Carla was very like her mother. The eldest, she was self-contained, confident and very beautiful. Like Ariana. Paola was a little scallywag, irritating her sister, vying with Carla for the affection of her mother. Just like herself. She gave Paola an extra hug. Carla did not seem to notice and Paola smiled at her radiantly, being the chosen one.

After breakfast on the terrace Maria, the maid, took the children to school and Ariana sat listening to her sister endlessly pour her heart out.

'I *should* have listened to you, I know, Ari. And Mama and Papa. But I was stubborn. I wanted to *show* you,' she explained, then shrugging, added, 'Show you what? I don't know!'

Ariana, puffing on her Marlboro, sipping her espresso, smiled and echoing Daniella's thought said, 'You're very like Paola. She's got something to prove. All the time. Perhaps you'll tell me about it and I can help her.'

'No amount of telling will change her, Ari. She'll have to learn for herself. But understanding her will help.'

'Mama used to say, "There's no stopping Dani when her mind's made up." But I hope poor Paola does not have to suffer as much as you have to find her truth.'

'It's an attitude. I was born seeing obstacles and having to overcome them.'

'And I either didn't see them or worked my way around them.'

Looking at her watch Daniella added, 'But here I am, keeping you from the gallery.'

'No, no. I only work four days a week now. Or three. I've learned to delegate. I have a wonderful guy there all the time. I trust him completely. The find of my life.'

'Oh. Is it doing well?' No good at small talk she could think of nothing else to say.

Ariana nodded. 'Mm. Very well. I only do what I want and still do extremely well. The stuff people buy!' She shook her head, casting her eyes to heaven. 'You wouldn't believe!'

'The girls are gorgeous, Ari. You must be very proud.'

'I am. Carla is an angel. Paola can be difficult. Carlo dotes.' Ariana squinted at her sister. 'And you? I'm sure you'd be a wonderful mother, Dani.'

'I told you. Rupert told me I was barren, but the doctor said . . .'

'You could always have proved him wrong *and* pleased him.' Ariana grinned.

'How?' Daniella asked, puzzled.

'You could have got pregnant by someone else, Dani,' Ariana smiled. 'That's what I would have done.'

Daniella stared at her round-eyed. 'You'd . . . Oh my God! It never even occurred to me.'

'I know. You're such an innocent, Dani. I bet Rupert's the only man you've ever been with.' Daniella blushed. She thought of Marcello, of that long slow passion, the overwhelming sensations, the resultant contentment. Ariana, seeing the colour suffuse her sister's face, laughed.

'Oh, you're so *modest*,' she said, thinking it was shyness. 'And that's so *old-fashioned*. You belong in Victorian times, you really do, Dani.'

If only you knew, Daniella sighed, but said nothing.

'Carlo is taking us out to dinner tonight,

pet,' Ariana was saying. 'I'll lend you a stunner. Or maybe you'd like to do some shopping?' She stood up. 'Let me make you a present. Get you a new dress. We'll go to the Via Condotti, have coffee in Caffè Greco and be back in time for the poppets' return from school. Okay?'

Daniella smiled. 'Okay,' she agreed, then leapt to her feet, full of sudden energy. 'Okay!'

CHAPTER NINE

Marcello Vestori reclined on the ornate chaise, his feet up, puffing on a cheroot, sipping a brandy. He was very relaxed there and Bella smiled looking at him. He was so delightfully handsome, a joy to watch. Not like the others.

The bed was tousled. It dominated the room, which was bathed in amber light. It was huge and covered in a crimson embroidered quilt.

Bella wore a wine velvet *robe de chambre*, open, draped loosely over her marble-white body. She lay, legs curled voluptuously, breasts unselfconsciously only half-concealed by the rich-textured garment, arms behind her head, leaning against the satin pillows.

Marcello always pleased her eyes. He was so gloriously beautiful, she reflected sadly, and it was time she cut the bonds that bound them

70

together.

Rudolpho Rizzi had sent his nephew to her to learn about love. Sex.

'It is important he learns to be a good lover. Expert at the making of love. It will change his life, make him and the women he loves very happy,' Rizzi had told her. 'He is a good boy. But impetuous. I want him to learn how to please a woman, please himself.'

Marcello had arrived on her doorstep and she'd had to be very strict with herself not to fall in love with him. It would have been all too easy and it probably would have destroyed her.

It was supposed to be only a few visits to Bella's third-floor apartment in the Piazza del Fiore but he kept coming back. Even when Bella told him in no uncertain terms, this was *finito*, still Marcello returned and she could never refuse him. Her other lovers, after all, were all so old.

Rudolpho Rizzi thought Marcello's visits to his mistress had stopped. He would be furious if he'd known that Marcello still hurried back to her. There was no one like her.

Still Rizzi was magnanimous. He was very happy for his mistress to instruct his young nephew in the arts of lovemaking, but enough was enough. Bella must not get too fond of romantic young men and had to remember on which side her bread was buttered.

Her steady customers, and there were only four of them, paid handsomely for her favours.

They all knew each other, belonged to the same social circle and jealously monopolised her. The Conte della Menase de Voluntrari, an old aristocrat well past the excitement of passion whose jaded palate she was capable of stirring, but not over-stimulating. He had a dicky heart. Generalissimo Raphael Donizetti, an old campaigner who at seventeen had served under Mussolini and who had somehow re-invented himself after the war, disclaiming all his previous activities and connections. Dominico Conti Romanazzi, an elegant, aged art dealer, Rome's most respected authority on Giotto. And Rizzi, her favourite.

Rizzi was the bucaneer member of the great shoe-making family and of the four who jealously guarded her for themselves it was he she liked best. So when he suggested, in strictest confidence, that she 'break young Marcello in', she agreed, albeit against her better judgement.

She had avoided gilded youth, aware she was drawn irresistably to it. She had become used to elderly lovers. A sensual woman who loved luxury, she had been dirt-poor and was determined to leave behind the rat-infested hovel she had been born into and carve a career out for herself. The kind of life she only sensed existed behind the high walls of the houses in Trastevere.

But she had no talent. She tried singing in a competition on TV Italia but was astute

72

enough to sense that she was making a fool of herself. The compère urged her tone-deaf carolling on and on, winking at the audience and she realised they saw her as a figure of fun; someone comic. She hated that. Then she got work as a waitress, then a receptionist and a salesgirl but always the boss or someone on the staff made overtures and she would be dismissed for refusing to co-operate. It was always her fault, they said, as if she could do anything about other people's behaviour. As if she could help it that her sex appeal was potent.

It was her one asset. Everywhere she went men were hot for her. She was taken up by an ageing film producer who arranged a film test for her, but the camera didn't like her and her sex appeal did not come across. She looked awkward and self-conscious on the screen.

It was the film producer who gave her the idea. He wanted her and was prepared to pay for her. What he did not want was to divorce his wife of thirty-seven years.

'She is the mother of my children. She is fifty-eight years old. It would not be honourable to dump her now, in her later years,' he tut-tutted. 'No, no, no. The men who do this are not real men. Not adult. They are frightened children, afraid of death. Besides, we have a history together, Gina and me. A lot of understanding, a lot of experiences that we share.'

He told her he'd buy her an apartment. 'In your own name. It will be yours. I will pay you . . .' he mentioned a sum that astonished her, it was so large, so generous. She was worth that much?

'Then I come to you. Tuesday, or Wednesday, or Thursday, or maybe all three. These days you will keep for me. You will know when to expect me, welcome me. The other days . . . he shrugged. 'What you do those days is none of my business, just as what I do those other days is none of yours. Okay? Other men? What you like. But . . .' he shook a finger at her, 'I think they must be men I know. Honourable men. Two or three. Not more. I do not want it to be like Fiumicino on a busy day. I do not want the apartment to become notorious. And clean. I want you to make sure you are clean.' He took out a card, flicked it with his thumb. 'This is a doctor. Specialises in that kind of thing. I expect you to consult him frequently. It is a business deal,' he said, and he put out his hand. 'Shake.'

She shook. She would have liked him to ask her to think it over. It distressed her that he was so sure she'd accept the offer, but he knew, obviously, that she would. A girl like her from the slums, no education, what choice did she have?

On the whole it had been easy. She enjoyed the things money bought; the fine foods, the wines, the beautiful designer clothes, the

74

expensive perfumes, the comfort. She knew that respectable people, the Roman matrons, despised and pitied her; and she knew she would never acquire their elegance, their taste, or their position and acceptance in society. She always went for the slightly gaudy, the exotic. But she was also aware that none of her contemporaries from the place she had come had made it thus far. Some had fallen by the wayside. A lot were drug addicts and alcoholics. Some were seen on the Via Appia nightly, shivering in their skimpy clothes, leaning into the cars that drew up, plying their trade on the boulevard. The same trade she was in, but at least she had a warm bed, a comfortable apartment. She did not delude herself.

Some still hung out in the slums, living with petty criminals and thieves who preyed on the stupid tourists, spending their vacations in jail. Few had the security she had. For that she was genuinely grateful.

And her clients were nice. Kindly. As she got to know them she got used to them and their little ways and was grateful to them.

Then Marcello Vestori came along. The film producer was long since dead. He'd had a heart attack in the bosom of his family in their country home in Tuscany where he spent every weekend.

Bella had not known whether or not to attend his funeral and had decided after much inner debate to go but lurk on the fringes, try not to be noticed. She had been very fond of him. Black garbed, black veiled, she had hovered near a tree in the cemetery, a little way apart from the mourners. But the producer's wife had left the graveside and gone to her where she stood. For a moment Bella had been fearful and flinched and stepped backwards, but there had been nothing but kindness in the widow's eyes.

'Thank you for being so good to my husband. For looking after him so well,' she had said. 'Come. Come with me,' and she led the mistress to the graveside with her, a hand firmly on her arm, patting it reassuringly.

Bella had wept then, touched and disarmed by the woman's gesture.

Bella had been seeing the Conte, who was a great friend of the producer, and when he died the Conte, with old-world courtesy, had asked her if perhaps she could find time to see the Generalissimo. He turned out to be a silver-haired old warrior who liked to talk about his grandchildren and the mistake he made as a boy. 'I was only eighteen. How was I to know?' They got on famously. He liked to take her out, show her off in public. 'Show them there's life in the old hound,' and he brought his friend Rudolpho. Rizzi became her favourite. He made her laugh and together they acted more like an old married couple who understood and forgave the flaws in each

76

other.

And then one day Rizzi asked the favour and the young and beautiful Marcello had entered her life.

That was twelve years ago. Marcello was now thirty and he still had not settled down or found himself a wife. It would not do. Time ticked on for men as well as women, as his mistress well knew and Bella loved him too much to see him waste his life on her.

'You will regret missing the best of life, *cara*,' she told him. 'You should be married, have children. It is normal.'

'But I don't want to be married,' he had said.

'You will wake up one day, an old man, no wife, no children, no grandchildren and you will hate me.'

'No, no, Bella. I could not hate you. Never.'

It was time, she knew, to set him free of her. He'd become used to her; she was a habit with him. He was comfortable with her and he was reluctant to move on, and she freely admitted to herself that she'd not been that eager to encourage him to leave her.

But very soon she realised he'd be so unused to any kind of real commitment, the commitment that marriage and children demanded that it would be too late and she would not have done the job Rizzi had asked her to do.

She looked at him, his long length lounging

on the chaise this May day and sighed again. The last thing she wanted was to dismiss him but she felt she had no choice.

'For the last time, Marcello, you must stop coming to me—'

To her surprise he interrupted her, 'Bella, I met a girl . . . a woman . . .'

She was surprised at the stab of jealousy that shot through her, fierce amd hot.

'She was . . .' he shrugged, 'a . . . *mystery* . . .'

'What do you mean, *cara*?'

She knew exactly what he meant. The one you fell in love with was, at first, always a mystery.

'What woman?' she asked dubiously.

He seemed lost in thought and did not answer. For a moment she wanted to shake him but she asked:

'When did you meet her?' Not where or with whom, but when. Had she been around a while? Weeks? Months? Did he think of her while he made love to his mistress? To her? All these questions she knew were ridiculous but they flashed into her mind anyway.

'What? Oh, yesterday,' he replied casually, his thoughts obviously elsewhere.

'You didn't say anything when you came here today.'

'No.' He seemed to shrug off some thought and added, 'I'll probably never see her again.' His voice was wistful.

'Why do you say that, *cara*?'

'It was . . .' he hesitated, 'a brief encounter.'
Then he frowned, 'Well, no, it wasn't . . .'
Hesitating again, he paused.

'Why don't you tell me about it?' she asked,
trying to keep her voice calm.

He told her. He explained about the bag-
strap and she laughed, then stopped abruptly
when she saw his face. He told her exactly
what had happened, their long talk, their
dinner and the resultant, and to him quite
unexpected, night of passion.

'She was so soft, Bella, so *inept*.' Bella
smiled wryly to herself. She had always
thought ineptitude a disadvantage and
expertise a trump card. Obviously she had
been wrong.

'It excited me, how clumsy she was. I guided
her and I felt so strong, so powerful, being able
to do that for her.' He glanced up at Bella,
who was pouring green tea from a samovar.

'I know,' she said, for that was what she had
felt with him.

'She had never before . . .' He looked at her
and grimaced.

'Poor girl,' Bella remarked, trying to control
her feelings. It was one thing to urge Marcello
to find himself a wife, another lover; another
to sit talking about her when he had.

But she understood about the girl. It had
been a long time before she too had had that
powerful and overwhelming climax. A very
long time. Perhaps, she decided, the first real,

79

full-blown, ecstatic tidal-wave had been with Marcello. Oh, she'd had what she thought of now as mini-climaxes, but not to that place of physical excitement and total abandon, that displacement of self when there was nothing in the world but this man and his body in yours. She had experienced that with her young lover, not with the others.

'Lucky girl, to have that, with you,' she murmured.

'Then she threw me out.' He muttered it and she thought she hadn't heard him aright.

'She *what*?' She stared at him incredulously

He glanced over his shoulder at her where she sat propped up by the pillows, drinking her tea.

'She threw me out, Bella. Couldn't wait to get rid of me.'

'Marcello! I cannot believe it.' She was genuinely mystified.

'I felt so . . . un-manned. I felt diminished, as if I counted for nothing. Was simply a machine,' he told her.

'Why would she do such a thing?' Bella mused. 'It is not as if she expected the husband back at any moment.' She smiled at him. 'She was afraid perhaps of what she had done,' she decided. 'That is it! She had never been unfaithful to this man . . . this horrible person she has run away from and she felt guilty.'

'You think so?'

'Yes, I do.'

'Then I must find her.'

'You love her? This girl?'

He frowned. Her heart ached at his concentration, not on her as it usually was, but on some private experience she was not party to.

'I don't know,' he said at last. 'I think of her all the time.'

'Just now?' she queried lightly, groaning inwardly. When you were with me? she longed to ask but did not say it aloud.

'I cannot get her out of my mind,' he said in an exasperated tone, suddenly jumping up.

She put the fragile cup and saucer on the small table beside her and rose also. She let the wine-coloured *robe de chambre* float loosely behind her as she moved sinuously towards him, her arms open to him.

'Once more before you go,' she whispered. She looked at him languidly, letting her fingers run over his cheek, the tip of her index finger caress his bottom lip, light as a butterfly's wings. She kissed him lightly on the corner of his mouth, then made to draw him to the bed. But he moved away from her.

'No, Bella. I haven't time,' he said abstractedly. 'I'd better get on.'

And then she knew she'd lost him.

CHAPTER TEN

They stood at the foot of the hospital bed, Gladys Weston and her son. It was neat and narrow, the covers smooth and tucked in pristine perfect around the body there.

'He was the greatest old bore,' she said bitterly.

'Hush, Mother, he can probably hear you.'

'I don't *care*. I've had *years* of him going on and on at me and now my bondage is over and all I can feel is relief.'

'But he needs you, Mother. He needs you now.'

'Well, he can jolly well do without me,' she said firmly and complacently.

Henry had had another stroke and the ambulance had brought him here into this brisk antiseptic place miles from Finchley. They said he'd be hospital-bound, or nursing-home material for a while. 'But we can't keep him here too long,' the harrassed matron told them. 'We need the bed.'

'You'll have to make other arrangements,' the doctor said. 'There's nothing more we can do at present.'

The doctor kept yawning hugely and had purple rings under his eyes. 'Like his mascara had slipped,' Gladys whispered to Rupert, who shot her a disapproving glance. This was neither the time nor the place to be facetious. In fact he disapproved of everything his mother was doing and saying, and most of all he disapproved of her appearance.

Now, in the hospital, she was wearing a most unsuitable dress that barely covered her thighs and over it a jacket of Auntie Janey's in bright orange that sat ill with her hennaed hair.

As his mother had no experience of make-up her attempts were fairly outlandish and Rupert felt deeply embarrassed by her. On being told that her husband was going home and she'd be expected to nurse him, in spite of the fact that he'd need constant care and was incontinent, she point-blank refused to be responsible for him.

'I will *not* do it. I will not be his nurse,' she cried. 'No, no, no.'

'But it's what's expected of you, Mrs Weston. Care in the Community, y'know. We'll get you extra help, of course ...' The matron paused.

'No, I won't do it,' Gladys said firmly. 'I won't. You can send me to prison but you can't make me. He'll have to go into a home and that's that. I'm *not*, repeat *not* going to be that man's slave any more. I hope that's clear.'

'Mother, you'll have to,' Rupert cried and the nurse nodded vehemently.

'No, I won't. I'll pay what I have to but I will not have that man in my home.' She was quite

83

adamant and Rupert simply did not know what to do.

The matron was not used to the kind of answers Gladys was giving. She expected people to keep to the script, but this lady was getting on her nerves.

'Oh, come now, Mrs Weston,' she snapped. 'That's what for better or for worse means, don't ye know.'

She knew better than any that the patients' nearest and dearest were often appalled at the thought of nursing their stricken relatives at home, but they usually concealed it. They hadn't the gall to refuse as brazenly as this woman.

'Don't you dare lecture me on my duties, Nurse,' Gladys chided. 'You haven't a clue. You don't know what I've had to put up with all these years. He's been a monster.'

The matron's eyes widened and they all three looked at Henry where he lay under the sheets, tubes sticking out of him and for a moment Rupert could have sworn his eyes opened and he thought he saw that wild, furious expression in them again. Then his lids drooped.

'I'm not looking after the old goat,' Gladys said with something of a smile on her face, and looking back at the matron she added, defiantly, 'So there!'

*　　　*　　　*

In the street his mother stood on tiptoe and kissed his cheek. He stepped back, startled. She'd never done that before, not even when he was off to boarding school.

'We weren't much use to you, Rupe, were we?' she asked.

'Oh Mother! Don't be silly.' He felt awkward and suspiciously close to tears, which horrified him.

'I'm not being silly. But last night, in that ward, with all those people dying and in pain I looked back over my life and realised I'd done it all wrong.' There was a depth of agony in her eyes that made him suck in his breath and turn away. He did not want to be burdened with her feelings just now, he had enough on his plate with his own.

People hurried in and out of the hospital, swirling around them in the bright sunshine. They stared at each other, two strangers, without words.

'You going home, Mother?' he asked eventually.

She shook her head, 'No. No, I'm going to Janey's,' she said and moved away and became, as he watched, part of the anonymous crowd.

CHAPTER ELEVEN

Rupert phoned Selina Wright. He had to talk to *someone* and as his father was *non compos mentis*, his mother a character-changed stranger, and his wife God knew where, Selina was the only one left.

Not that he'd ever really spoken to her before, any more than he'd spoken to Daniella, but he kept thinking about the conversation in the Rat and Parrot and some of the things Selina had said to him on that occasion.

She answered promptly, 'Yeah?'

'It's Rupert.'

'The Neanderthal man! What do you want?' Her voice was sassy and he nearly told her to go to hell. Then thinking better of it, with unaccustomed humility and complete loss of pride he told her, 'I need to talk.'

He'd heard it repeated many times on the telly, in soaps and chat shows, and he'd always despised the people who would come out with it. I need to talk. Ugh! Undignified and embarrassing revelations about themselves. Too, too shaming. His father had told him it was simply not done.

'Keep it to yourself, laddie,' he said. 'Terribly bad form, spilling your guts out to anyone.'

Well, his father, it seemed, had been wrong about a lot of things and Rupert was desperate.

So Rupert said it now and he meant it. The need was acute.

'I need to talk.'

'You, Rupe? Oh my God!' She sounded derisive but he persisted.

'Yes, me!' he cried shrilly, annoyed by this banter. 'Me. My life is falling apart and I don't know what to do.' It was a cry from the heart, agony to admit, but he got it out. Selina did not seem the least impressed.

'It had to happen sooner or later, old chap. Your behaviour is so prehistoric, it was inevitable.' She paused and he could think of nothing to say. 'What do you expect me to do?' she asked.

'Help me, please.'

There, it was out. The great self-sufficient macho guy like a child, helplessly defeated, begging for assistance.

There was a pause, then she said much more seriously, 'Where are you?'

'I'm at King's Cross.'

'Christ! Well, I won't ask what you are doing there. Okay. I'll see you in the Rat and Parrot in an hour.'

He put down the phone, so relieved he nearly sank to the ground in the telephone booth. He'd tell her all about it and she'd know what to do because he sure as hell didn't.

87

He'd always disliked and feared Selina Wright but she was a very strong person, incisive and sure of herself, and just now he needed someone who could give him some idea what to do. How to behave. About Daniella. About his mother and father. It was all getting out of hand, uncontrollable, and if there was one thing that terrified Rupert more than anything else it was not being in control.

He went on the circle line to Temple, got off and walked. He felt agitated and kept muttering to himself as he strode nervously along the crowded pavement. How in God's name had he arrived at this point in his life? It had all seemed so simple before Dani's dramatic departure. He had a family, familiar and loved, a father whose advice he respected, a mother who looked after his every need. He had a beautiful wife who did as she was told, like it said in the Bible, ministered unto him, was a helpmeet to him. And he had a career at which he excelled. At which he was feared. Defence councils quaked before him. Judges respected him.

Suddenly, overnight it seemed, it was all gone. He'd made a fool of himself before Judge Dempsey, Dani had stormed out, his father had disintegrated and his mother had become a virtual stranger, and not one that he particularly liked.

He entered the bar and saw Selina and felt relief flood over him. His shoulders, which he'd had hunched up, relaxed and he hurried towards her. She had her back to him but there was no mistaking that shining tangle of hair. His heart rose and for some reason he was filled with the certainty that everything would be all right.

He sat down opposite her, looking at her expectantly. She laughed.

'What's the problem, Rupe?' she asked buoyantly. He was a little miffed by her attitude. She should be like his mother used to be: all attention. She should take him seriously.

'Please don't call me Rupe,' he said peevishly.

'Oh, my dear!' she cried. 'You've given up the right to demand Rupert since your débâcle the other day.'

'Anyone can make a mistake.' He was being pettish and he knew it. He seemed to have lost the ability to sound his usual dogmatic self.

'Not of that magnitude,' she said with cruel accuracy and he wondered why he wanted so much to confide in her. She was distinctly unsympathetic. 'Everyone is talking about you,' she cried happily. 'Beastie Bestwick walks and who set him free? Why, Rupert Bear!'

'Oh, shut up, you bitch!' he hissed angrily.

She suddenly became absolutely still. She looked at him with calm eyes, so cold they could have frozen hell over.

'Never, *never* call me that,' she said softly,

distinctly, almost whispering and he knew she meant it. There was absolutely no leeway here. He remembered Daniella's frozen face, but she had cowed and taken it, which made him feel better. But he was acutely aware that he could take no such liberty with Selina Wright.

He cleared his throat nervously. This was the reason he disliked her so much. She made him feel small, so *wrong*, yet here he was, abjectly seeking her help.

'Okay,' he said contritely.

'*I* am not Daniella,' she added firmly.

'I said okay.'

There was a silence and he looked at her. She was waiting.

'Well?' she prompted, 'How can I help?'

He wished suddenly that he was anywhere but here in the golden gloom of the Rat and Parrot. He decided death would be preferable, then cleared his throat. She further disconcerted him by saying as he did so, 'You're not in court now, Rupe.'

'I don't know what to do,' he admitted. 'Daniella's left me and I think she's gone to her sister in Italy. But I don't know what to do.'

'Go after her,' she told him instantly.

'But her sister hates me. I've never really been abroad.' He winced as he remembered the honeymoon. 'Only once.'

'And you didn't like it,' she smiled. 'Xenophobic as well!'

'Please come with me.' He blurted it out without thinking. Selina spluttered over her drink.

'With you?' she asked incredulously.

'Yes,' he said.

She'd carve her way through the mystifying ritual of check-in, passport control. She'd be *au fait* with that baggage check where he'd scared himself to death by suddenly going off, beeping loudly as he passed under the portal and they body-searched him as if he were a terrorist or gangster. Selina would be travelwise. She'd do all that petrifying stuff, know which queue to join, checking for where and when their flight went from and what time. Things that threw him into complete confusion. He could eyeball a murderer in court with confidence but he found it terrifying to find the right departure gate. Selina would know about boarding. Everyone else seemed to be familiar with the working of airports and he felt a complete fool being unwilling to reveal his ignorance. All the things that had frightened and unmanned him on his honeymoon, that he'd found daunting, she would deal with as a matter of course.

He sat looking at her expectantly in the dim cosy light. He thought he hadn't heard aright when she said brightly, 'Okay.'

'What?'

'I said okay.'

'But . . . can you really?'

She laughed again, that infuriating, confident laugh.

'What you didn't know, Rupe, is that I'm on leave at this moment. Why do you think I was at home when you called?' She made a face, then answered her own question, 'Silly me! Of course you didn't even realise! You're so wrapped up in your own troubles that you can't see beyond the end of your nose.'

'I'm sorry,' he said.

'And so you should be! God . . . I might be up to my neck in shit for all you'd suss.'

'But you aren't!'

'No, I'm not. I'm foot-loose and fancy free. Now, go to the bar and get me another vodka and tonic. I need another drink. I think I must have lost my mind, agreeing to this.'

He did as she asked. He realised that he'd forgotten to offer her one and she'd been nursing the drink she'd had when he'd joined her.

When he returned, having bought himself a beer, with her vodka, she told him, 'All expenses paid, Rupert. This will cost you. And I don't promise results.'

'What do you mean?'

She leaned forward. 'What I mean is, I get to go to Italy, you pay all expenses: flight, hotel, food, and in return I do all I can, cross-my-heart, to help you, but there are no guarantees. I'm not going to try to coax, manipulate, entice Daniella back into your bed, so unless you've got all that clearly in that thick skull of yours, the deal is off.'

He had no option but to accept her terms and though normally he would have been outraged, just then he was only too happy to agree. Anything was better than the limbo he was struggling in. He'd have paid her a fee on top of the expenses if she'd demanded it but happily for him she didn't.

'When do we go?' she asked cheerfully.

'As soon as possible,' he said. 'Does that suit you?' There was a *soupçon* of sarcasm in his voice and she glanced at him and grinned.

'Yeah. I told you. I'm on leave. I was at a loose end.' A remote expression flitted across her face, 'Malcolm and I have split up. We were to go to Kenya, on safari, but that's off now . . .'

'Malcolm Molyneux?' he asked breathlessly. '*Malcolm*? You and he were never . . .'

'Oh Rupert, you old head-in-sand. Don't you hear anything? Don't you *observe*? Yes, we were an item. Everyone knew,' she smiled at him ruefully, 'except you, it seems. Well,' she sighed and pushed back her hair, 'it's over now and *you* know how painful that can be.'

'Uhuh. But Daniella and I aren't over,' he protested.

She looked at him as if he was an insect. 'You might be surprised about Daniella,' she said. 'But don't you realise, you little toad, that I've just told you I've separated from the man I

93

loved and you've not even communicated one second's sympathy?' She leaned back in her chair. 'You really are the most self-centred person I've ever met, Rupe, you know that? I feel I should give up, I really do.'

'Don't, please, call me Rupe. I *hate* it.'

'Okay, Rupe,' she twinkled at him maliciously.

He could see she was right. It had not even occurred to him to commiserate with her over her broken affair. He realised belatedly that he'd not been considering her at all.

'I'm quite pleased, actually, to get away,' she was saying. 'Run away from the mess.' She tossed back her drink and rose. 'Okay, Rupe. Get the tickets and phone me and I'll be ready to take off instantly.'

She left the pub purposefully and he stared after her, wondering why he felt so relieved. Content, almost. Even though she insisted on calling him that awful diminution of his name and wouldn't do as he asked. He'd never tolerate that in Daniella. He would not put up with such impertinence. But Selina was not his wife, thank God. He thought briefly of Malcolm Molyneux and had a sudden vision of him and Selina locked naked in an embrace. Appalled by the image that flashed across his mind he shuddered and put the thought firmly aside. Everything, he believed, would be all right now that Selina Wright was coming with him to Italy.

All his problems would be solved. Somehow.

CHAPTER TWELVE

'I'm going to Rome, Mother,' he said into the phone.

'When?' Her voice sounded faint.

'Tomorrow. Noon flight BA to Fiumicino.'

As if it mattered. His mother seemed to be in another world entirely.

'Have you changed your mind about Father?' he asked.

'No, dear. He's going into St Vincent's this evening. I've made arrangements. He'll be comfortable there.'

'But Mother . . .'

'There's no point in arguing, Rupert. My mind is made up. You're lucky,' her voice sounded suddenly strong, 'to be going to Italy.'

'But you hate . . .'

'No, Rupert. I know what you're going to say. But it's not true. *I* don't hate foreign countries. Your father hates foreign travel. Not me. I only said so for a quiet life.' Then her voice faded again and he could hear what he assumed was Auntie Janey's voice in the background, then a whispered exchange, then, 'Yes, Janey, I'll be with you in a mo', then into the phone, 'Goodbye, dear,' and a click and the connection cut.

He didn't know where St Vincent's was and he wanted to see his father before he went away, so he set out immediately to get to the hospital before his father left.

He didn't like the hospital. It was such a large, sprawling place. He took the left turn to the ward but got lost and had to retrace his steps. Kafka, he thought, would be at home here in these corridors. No one paid a blind bit of notice to his coming and going. Doctors passed by talking earnestly to each other and nurses scurried past too preoccupied to be asked directions.

He eventually found the ward but the bed his father had occupied was empty. He felt suddenly cold and tired. Lonely. He'd been deserted by the only people in his life that mattered to him. There was no one there, and God help him he needed them now.

He hurried down the ward to where a nurse was taking an elderly patient's temperature.

'Where is Mr Weston? He was in that bed.' Pointing to where his father had been. But she put her finger to her lips and told him in a cheerful whisper that she didn't know where his father was. 'Sorry,' she said and returned briskly to her patient.

He went to the door marked 'Staff', knocked and opened it.

'Does anyone in this place know where Mr Weston is?' he enquired in his most astringent advocate's voice.

The air was thick with cigarette smoke. A group of nurses, male and female, sat about drinking coffee, chatting.

'Who?' one of them asked indifferently.

'Mr Weston?'

'Oh him! He's waiting in the hall,' someone at the back of the room called.

'Which hall?' he snapped.

'The one beside Jane Austen.' A pretty, rosy-cheeked nurse emerged from a pall of smoke and stood, her arms stretched out, one hand on each side of the doorframe barring his way. 'Between Jane Austen and Nelson Mandela,' she said. 'Down the stairs and turn right.' And she closed the door firmly in his face.

He was too distraught to make an issue of it. He ran down the stairs, followed the arrows to Jane Austen and there, in the hall, sitting forlornly quite by himself in that vast place, silhouetted against the sun-drenched world outside, he found his father, waiting.

He did not move or seem to recognise Rupert. He stared blankly into the distance as if into another dimension. Rupert passed his hand up and down and across his father's eyes but he did not blink.

'Father. Father, it's Rupert.' No reply, just that vacant stare. 'Oh Father.' Rupert sank to his knees and laid his head on his father's knee. He felt the sting of tears behind his eyes.

His father would hate it if he cried, Rupert knew that. He blinked furiously. 'Oh Father!' Once again no reaction. His father's hand lay lifeless and relaxed on his knee and Rupert picked it up and pressed it to his cheek. Then he dropped it guiltily as he realised that his father would hate that too.

'Rupert! What on earth are you doing?' His mother's voice sounded loud in the echoing silence of the huge hall. 'You know your father would hate such a maudlin display. That's what he called emotion. Maudlin.'

Her voice pulled him together. His father, it was only too true, would recoil from such a demonstration of affection. He wondered briefly what Selina Wright would think of that.

He stood up. 'Are you taking him to that place, Mother?' he asked.

She nodded briskly. 'Yes. And don't call it *that place*. It's called St Vincent's.'

'Suppose he doesn't like it there?'

'Nonsense. Of course he'll be okay. He doesn't know day from night, Rupert, for heaven's sake. Look at him.'

'We don't know that he can't hear every word we say.'

'Well, I don't believe it for a moment. And even if he does, hard cheese, tough. What can we do about it?'

'Mother, but you can't! It's a terrible thing to do . . .'

She turned on him furiously. 'Well then,'

she cried, whirling the wheelchair roughly around, making him jump, pushing the handles into his solar plexus, 'you take charge of him then. *You* feel so strongly, *you* do it. You be responsible for him. *You* nurse him.'

Then, as he swiftly, almost automatically, swivelled the wheelchair back to her, his mother cried, 'Well, Rupert? What is it to be? You want him looked after, but you won't do it. It has to be me, does it? Just like your father. Wanting, no, *demanding* things done but never doing those things yourself. Making *me* do them. Whenever there was a duty or a chore he always said, "This is your job, Gladys". Well, I've had enough of it. Quite enough! So,' she cocked her hennaed head to one side, looking at him brightly. 'Well, Rupert? You want him?'

He shook his head feebly and Gladys waved towards the automatic doors and the waiting car outside.

'In that case . . .' she said and began to wheel Henry out.

CHAPTER THIRTEEN

Daniella relaxed a little in her sister's company. Everyone seemed to know Ariana. In shops, on the streets, they all greeted her, arms flung wide, kisses on both cheeks, loud exclamations of affection. She refused to allow Daniella to use her credit card and insisted she be allowed to spoil her sister by treating her. She kitted her out in style, in peach and violet, pale lime and that yellow she insisted suited Dani so well.

Daniella had to agree the new colours looked well on her and she *felt* different. She felt in some sense released, as if bonds had been broken, which of course they had. She felt as if she'd been carrying a huge burden and she'd been miraculously relieved of it, and although she'd had no alcohol she felt a little drunk. She realised, as she walked slightly behind her sister, following her down the Via Condotti, struggling with her shiny designer bags, that she'd been feeling intoxicated ever since she'd walked out of the house in Lansdowne Road. The same feeling she had when Rupert permitted her to have a second gin and tonic. On those occasions she'd experienced a heady sensation and her limbs felt liquid, her head in the clouds somewhere above her, and she was warm and cosy inside, and content, walking on air, certain that nothing could ever hurt her again. That was how she felt in Rome now, with her sister. Nothing could hurt her, bruise her. Everything was all right.

Except the thought of Marcello, which every now and then popped unwarranted into her head, making her wince, so she firmly and immediately squashed it.

No room for that memory, no room for pain.

They had lunch on the way back to the villa. They sat in the ivy-covered courtyard of the restaurant under an umbrella in the warm somnolent day and the bees buzzed above the adjacent olive grove. They ate salad and fish and drank red wine and laughed and chatted or were silent as the mood held them.

Daniella reversed her opinion of Ariana. Her sister never threw unpleasant facts at her, never accused her of having been silly, never blamed her for the mess she'd gotten herself into. She was understanding and compassionate and Daniella realised that she herself had written the script for her sister. She had decided how her sister would react, she had attributed opinions and conclusions to Ariana that were totally false and existed only in *her* mind.

'I thought you'd blame me. Despise me,' she said.

'Oh no, Dani. Whatever gave you that idea?'

'Well, you always seemed fed up with me on the phone.'

'I was fed up with *him*. I love you, Dani, and I knew he was hurting you. I wanted you out of there and I thought I could spur you on. Tough love!' She leaned back in her chair and lit a cigarette. 'Well, you've taken the all-important step now, little sister, and that's a huge relief, I can tell you. But,' she looked intently at Daniella, 'you've got my full support no matter what you decide. Even if . . .' she rolled her eyes heaven-ward, 'though God forbid!'

'Thank you, Ari. That means so much to me.'

They drank espressos and Ariana insisted on paying the bill and they went out into the hot sunshine and drove back to the villa.

The children came home and the sisters sat on the shaded terrace and drowsed in the afternoon heat. The chorus of cicadas crescendoed as they listened to the children's tales of woe, clucked over them as they drank their milk and laughed with them as they discarded bit by bit the tensions of school and slowly became Ariana's *bambini* again.

'We'll be leaving about eight-thirty this evening,' Ariana told her. 'Wear the strawberry silk with the jacket. It's a bit formal, this place, but you'll like it.'

That seemed fine to Daniella who wondered at her new-found confidence, her lack of apprehension about going to a strange, possibly daunting, venue.

They bathed the children who shrieked with laughter and splashed about and slipped out of their grasp delightedly. Maria towelled Carla dry while Ariana and Daniella chased Paola around the room, rubbing her dry when they could get their hands on her.

The sun went down and the evening cooled. They tucked the girls up in bed, leaving only the night-light burning. Ariana told her girls a story about shoes and silver dresses and a pretty girl and a prince finding her and everything being all right in the end but they fell asleep half-way through.

'They look like little angels,' Daniella whispered, gazing down at their flushed faces, their soft tousled hair. Paola's thumb had fallen out of her mouth which, like a rose-bud at dawn, was half-open, and Carla had a starfish hand curled on her forehead. Ariana smiled fondly.

'They are so precious, Dani,' she said. 'My life. My treasures.' And the sisters tiptoed out and all was quiet.

CHAPTER FOURTEEN

'Hi, chuck.' It was Selina's voice right behind him in Heathrow Airport, using, he thought, a stupid Liverpool accent that she didn't imitate very well.

But he jumped. 'Don't do that!' he cried sharply.

'If everything I do drives you potty, Rupe, I can't for the life of me think why you want me along!'

'Neither can I!' he snapped back. 'You are the most irritating woman I've ever met.'

'And you are the most foul-tempered, sexist, selfish man I've ever met,' she retorted.

They walked side by side to the check-in. He ushered her to the fore, partly because it was good manners but mainly because he felt insecure and he wanted her to lead the way.

He'd bought a smart case the day before and he'd tried to rough it up a bit but it simply looked scratched. He'd not known what to pack either. Never intending to travel he'd not paid any attention to what the climate anywhere outside England might be like. He supposed Italy to be hot and hoped his chinos, his Ralph Lauren jeans, his linen suit bought for freak heatwaves in London would suffice. He was unsure and therefore touchy.

Selina looked ultra-smart, very fetching in a cream linen suit and white body, dark brown leather accessories. She had a Panama hat perched nonchalantly on her tousled head. She was, moreover, obviously *au fait* with all the flight procedures which she performed automatically and he sulkily but gratefully allowed her to lead the way through passport control, baggage check to the departure lounge.

In the lounge she stood a moment looking up at the monitor, tapping her watch-face. 'Let me see. We've about twenty minutes. I want to get some duty-free scent. Meet you at gate 14,' and to his consternation she disappeared into the supermarket.

Looking around he eventually found indicators to the gate but then discovered it was the wrong airline flight to Rome. They were going BA and this was Alitalia. So he had to return down endless passages, back through some check mechanisms and more endless corridors and once more through the check-in he had already been through, meeting on the way irate officials who informed him that he couldn't do this and that.

When he reached the correct gate Selina was looking for him and she greeted him with an angry, 'Where the hell have you been?'

He was feeling irritable and gauche so he glared at her. She stuck her face close to him, 'Smell,' she cried. 'Nice?'

'What?' he cried angrily.

'Nice pong.' She giggled, waving her wrist under his nose. 'Think it suits me?'

'Yes. Listen Selina, this is a *serious* mission. You are being frivolous and I'd like you to remember I'm trying to get my wife back. It's *not* a holiday! Understand?'

She sniffed, 'What do you want me to do? Carry on like I was at a funeral?' She pulled a long face, then grinned at him impishly, 'Oh, come on, Rupert. You're just in a bad mood and you're taking it out on me. It's not going to help, me being serious, having my church face on, you being grumpy. It's not going to get

Daniella back, is it?'

He didn't reply. He was getting antsy again, wondering why they were waiting, unwilling to ask her why they had to hang about again.

'Why do you want her back anyway?' Selina asked. 'Are you sure that you do?'

He looked at her, startled. 'Of course I do!' he cried loudly, then glanced around sheepishly, realising that people had turned, looked up from their books and newspapers, their magazines at the vehemence of his protest.

'Of course I do,' he said in a lower tone. 'What do you think?'

She shrugged. 'Dunno. Couldn't be hurt pride? Could be she had the cheek to do something you didn't sanction.' She laughed. 'Some men, Rupert, never get over their wives walking out on them. And you know why? Not because they love them but because their pride is hurt. If their wives returned to them they'd be satisfied but lose interest instantly and begin divorce proceedings *tout de suite*. In my considered opinion . . .' She clapped her hand to her mouth and giggled. 'Sorry. There I am again, sounding legal.'

'I don't know what you're getting at,' Rupert muttered angrily. 'I love my wife and I want to get her back.'

'If you love her and she's unhappy with you,' she glanced at him sideways, 'wouldn't the thing be to let her go?'

'She doesn't know what she wants. You don't understand, Selina, Daniella can't manage without me.' This line of conversation was making him acutely uncomfortable and he wished to heaven she'd stop.

'She seems to have managed very well just recently. She's run away and covered her tracks so no one knows where she is.'

'Oh shut up . . .' He nearly added bitch but caught her eye and stopped himself in time.

'I'm not Daniella,' she said quietly. 'You call me anything, *anything* inappropriate and I'll leave you *instantly*. I'll walk away and you won't see me again. Understand?'

He swallowed and bit his lip. She meant it, he had no doubt about that.

'If she really loves you she'll come back to you,' Selina said in a kinder tone, then, picking up *Vanity Fair* she quite firmly cut him out and became absorbed in what she was reading.

They sat for a while in silence. Rupert wished now he had something to read. A uniformed man, handsome, tanned and silver-haired, came striding past the waiting crowd talking to a younger man. Both were all braid and peaked hats pulling carryons, obviously the captain and co-pilot, Rupert decided, gazing enviously at them. They were so nonchalantly confident, top-dog here, cutting a cool dash, no waiting like penned cattle in a bunch, but swanning through and out, special, privileged.

'Oh help! Oh no! Oh dear God!' he yelled suddenly.

Selina, startled by his tone looked up from her magazine.

'What's the matter?' she asked mildly.

'I don't believe it! Oh no, it can't be . . .'

'*What is it, Rupert?*' She was becoming irritated.

'It's my mother!'

Making her way past the stewardess at the entrance to gate 14 was a figure in an orange two-piece with hennaed hair and outrageous make-up. The orange skirt was handkerchief-sized and revealed two bony knees. The woman looked around the crowd and when she spotted him she waved violently and made a beeline over to where Rupert and Selina sat near the exit to the plane.

They were calling the seat numbers and in a chaotic jumble and all at the same time Rupert Weston tried to hear what they were announcing, understand what was expected of him now, whether he was supposed to board or not, introduce his mother to Selina and vice versa, find his boarding pass, figure out where his seat number was on it, explain to his mother what Selina was doing accompanying him to Rome, and find out what his mother thought she was doing boarding this plane with them.

It was, he decided gloomily, going to be a very bumpy ride.

CHAPTER FIFTEEN

'She was never right for him,' Gladys Weston was telling Selina. 'It was his father's doing. He was so against the match, because she is half-Italian and Henry didn't approve of that, so *of course* he had to marry her.'

He'd been prepared for Selina's scorn. He'd been trying as they sorted out their seats to apologise for his mother's terrible appearance and make excuses for her, but to his vast surprise Selina and his mother seemed to hit it off extremely well.

'Personally,' his mother was saying, 'I think Italians are exciting. Very foreign. Exotic.'

Gladys was confiding cosily in Selina in the seats directly in front of him on the aircraft. He'd been shunted behind them, the steward asking Rupert to take the seat allocated to his mother so that she could sit beside Selina. She ignored his demands that he needed to sit beside his friend so they could plan, that he had to talk to her.

'Well, that can all wait,' his mother said comfortably. 'I have a lot to ask this young lady.' Then to Selina, 'I never meet any of his friends. Never. He doesn't introduce me or bring them home to the house. Or ask me to his either. Of course that was his father's doing, *again*,' she explained. 'We lived with his father under a very strict regime. Almost Nazi. You wouldn't credit, my dear. His father did not encourage the making of friends.' Her voice was bitter. 'His father, Selina, was against *fun*.'

'Ah!' Selina raised an eyebrow and glanced back at him. 'So that explains it.'

'Anything that could be called enjoyable, his father was very firmly against. Not a nice man, my husband.'

'Mother!' He leaned forward, trying to stop her, to put a brake on these terrible revelations, but it was no use. Kept silent for all these years his mother was unstoppable.

Rupert leaned back and closed his eyes. He felt nervous and at a complete disadvantage. By closing his eyes he could try to cut out the nagging anxieties that threw him into confusion.

He drifted off, somewhere, he was not sure exactly where, but a place of peace, it seemed. Not anywhere he'd ever been before.

He was beside a lagoon, an unreal aquamarine pool. It was dotted with waterlilies and little waves undulated and curled around the green banks that circled the pool. He could hear the splashing of falling water and looking around saw that beside him a waterfall cascaded in perpetual shining motion, the silver iridescent drops catching the rays of the sun which slanted in golden spears into the lake.

110

It was so tranquil there that he smiled and sighed and lay back to enjoy the serene beauty of the place.

As he did so he was startled by a laugh and sitting up straight he saw Selina rise from the other side of the lagoon, emerge from the light-blue waters like Botticelli's Venus, stark naked. She did not even have the goddess's wraps of veiling partly to conceal her nudity.

He sucked in his breath, tried to close his eyes, but they were already tightly closed. He stared at her as she lifted her arm and beckoned him seductively . . .

Just at that moment his mother's voice cut harshly across his consciousness.

' . . . But he's not irretrievably ruined.' She was talking, he realised, about him and she sounded *loud*, as if she was trying to top the noise of the plane's engines.

'Oh, I'm aware of that, otherwise I wouldn't be here.' Selina sounded matter-of-fact.

'His father stuffed his head full of atrocious beliefs and incorrect ideas,' Gladys was telling her, 'but I think he can be coaxed out of those utterly Victorian concepts. But you've got to be firm,' she warned.

Selina nodded in agreement. 'I've discovered that already,' she told his mother.

He felt a sinking sensation and heard the steward announce something about fastening seat-belts and putting the seat in an upright position and realised they were going to land.

There was no stopping events now, he realised dully, no halting what happened next. They were committed now. Out of the airport, into the taxi, the next stop, Ariana's, where he was sure he would find his wife.

What then? Totally bemused, Rupert had to admit to himself he had not the faintest idea.

CHAPTER SIXTEEN

The dining room in the Excelsior was old-world grand; glittering chandeliers, white napery, tinkling glass and silver service.

The *maître d'* greeted Carlo and his party effusively, welcoming them, leading them to their table.

Carlo set out to make Daniella feel relaxed and at her ease.

'You look *bella, bellissima,*' he told her, smiling in that appreciative way Italian men had. 'If I had not married Ariana, I would have had to marry you, Dani.'

Ariana had told her, 'Italian men adore women. Englishmen are terrified of them.'

They sat around the table and Daniella allowed herself to thaw out. She could not remember when last she had been to a place like this: discreet service, starched white table-linen, superb wine and food. She expanded under Carlo's charm, the relaxing influence of the wine and the knowledge that she did, in fact, look beautiful. When she caught sight of herself in the gilded-frame mirrors she hardly recognised herself. That glamorous made-over girl reflected there was surely not the brow-beaten Mrs Weston of Lansdowne Road, Holland Park? And it was not simply gayer clothes and a new hairstyle. She had lost that dejected, guilty demeanour and there was a sparkle now in her eyes and a colour in her cheeks and a joyous lift to her heart that shone forth making her beautiful.

They ate a delicious plate of roasted peppers of all colours, shining crimson, canary yellow, orange and emerald green, aubergines and courgettes, which reminded the girls of their father's trattoria in Greek Street and they got to telling Carlo stories from the past, about their childhood in Soho and their father's hysterical concern that they didn't see some of the racier venues advertised in the sex shops in that neighbourhood.

'Soho is pock-marked with these places, one between every few respectable businesses.'

'They were hard to miss,' Daniella said, 'And Papa was terrified we'd see something we shouldn't. He used to cover our eyes when we passed by. But we peeked, didn't we, Ari?'

'We never saw anything though,' Ariana laughed. 'The adult sex shops weren't allowed to advertise or put salacious pictures outside, so we were always disappointed.'

'Going to Mass on Sunday, to the Italian church,' Daniella giggled, 'Mama whisking us past . . . remember . . . what was it called, Ari?'

They were laughing, relaxed in that miasma of shared memories. Ariana pressed her napkin to her mouth as they waited for their second course, when Daniella looked across the restaurant and saw him. Marcello. Standing in the entrance.

Her heart stopped a split second, then recommended its tattoo, but faster, much faster.

She stared at him and he, glancing around the room, suddenly spotted her.

They gazed at one another, a long, still, suspended moment. The sounds of the restaurant seemed to Daniella suddenly stilled and the whole place held its breath.

Marcello said something to the *maitre d'*, nodded towards Daniella and to her horror strode purposefully through the room towards their table.

'Marcello!'

Carlo rose and the men embraced, greeting each other enthusiastically, slapping each other's shoulders.

Daniella sat in turmoil. She could feel her heart racing, her throat dry up, her stomach lurch.

'I think you know my wife, Ariana,' Carlo was saying.

'We've met.' Ariana, smiling, held out her

114

hand which Marcello raised briefly to his lips.

'And this is my sister-in-law, Daniella.'

Oh, please let him not say anything, Daniella prayed, and to her relief Marcello merely bowed and said, 'I'm delighted.'

'You must join us Marcello, *pronto*,' Carlo decided. He clicked his fingers, organising the waiters who were rushing about, setting another place, bringing another chair and all the while Ariana was watching her sister and the newcomer intently.

There was something palpable in the air; something she could not define, could not put her finger on, was happening or had happened between these two.

She quickly tried to remember Marcello Vestori's position: unmarried, scion of a brilliantly successful designer-shoe manufacturer, and mentally congratulated herself on her choice of restaurant.

'You two have met?' Ariana asked astutely and for a moment Daniella felt faint.

Marcello answered, 'Yes. In a way. I think your sister stayed the other night in the same hotel I did.' He said it lightly, casually. 'I saw Daniella in the foyer.'

Ariana wanted to say, 'Oh, made an impression, did she?' but refrained and held her peace. It was clear to her that there was more here than met the eye.

'May I say that you look very beautiful this evening,' Marcello was saying to Daniella.

Then he glanced at Ariana, 'And you too, of course.'

But Daniella was now staring, her face a mask of horror, towards the entrance. She had gone horribly pale and was making a faint protesting sound and, lifting her finger like the Ancient Mariner, she was pointing, manners forgotten, at the door.

Marcello turned and saw there, standing uncertainly, a harrassed-looking man, an extraordinary-looking older woman with orange hair, and a stunningly glamorous female who was looking about her with an arrogant, almost disdainful expression on her beautiful face.

'It's Rupert!' Ariana gave a little shriek. 'Help! It's Rupert and his mother.'

'And Selina Wright,' Daniella breathed. 'Holy cow, what's she doing here?'

'Oh my God, Maria must have told them where to find us.'

Rupert had spotted them and was waving in their direction. Next thing, the party moved towards their table.

'I hope there's not going to be a scene,' Ariana muttered.

'Leave this to me,' Carlo said masterfully and as they neared he extended a hand and smiling broadly he cried, 'Rupert! How nice to see you.'

'Signor, the table is for four, I really . . .' the *maître d'* was trying to explain. 'There is no more room, Signor, no room to be comfortable.' He spread his hands helplessly.

Rupert was staring at his wife.

'What have you done to yourself, Daniella?' he asked.

'It suits you, Daniella, whatever you did,' Selina remarked appreciatively. Rupert glared at her but undaunted she continued, 'I'm Selina Wright, everyone. Come to see World War Three doesn't break out.'

'And why should it?' Carlo asked benignly and glanced meaningfully at Rupert. 'We are civilized people here, I'm sure, and know how to behave. We are not hooligans.'

Rupert drew in a deep breath. Gladys pushed forward past her son and leaned towards Daniella who shrank back apprehensively, expecting her mother-in-law to read the riot act.

'Well done, Daniella,' she said, much to her daughter-in-law's astonishment. 'About time you got out from under.' And with that she sat down in the chair Carlo had vacated, looked around the table and remarked, 'Well, this is very nice, very nice indeed.' She turned to Rupert. 'My husband, your father, Rupert, is an ignorant man. He led me to believe that all foreigners were barbarians. Well . . .' Glancing around the room at the chandeliers, the mirrors, the exquisite flower arrangement in the centre of the room, she continued, 'He did not know his arse from his elbow, now did he?'

117

'Mother, shut up. Daniella, you come with me instantly. You've been a very naughty girl, worrying me like that. I didn't know where you were. It's all been most upsetting for me, really it has.'

Selina whispered fiercely, 'Oh Rupe, that's not the way.'

Daniella rose unsteadily to her feet. 'This is horrible,' she cried.

'I'll take care of her,' Rupert hurried to her side. 'Come with me.'

'No, I won't,' Daniella protested petulantly. 'Leave me alone.'

'Good on you, girl,' Selina whooped and Rupert glared at her. 'Hush,' he hissed. 'Don't you say another word.'

'Don't you dare tell me to hush,' Selina said imperiously to him while Marcello, who had risen also, asked Daniella quietly, 'What do you want, Daniella? What you want is what is important.' Daniella was looking at him in a bemused way. 'I'd like to talk to you, if you'll let me,' he said softly.

'Aha!' Ariana muttered. 'I knew it.'

'Rupert has come all this way to take you home, Dani,' Gladys said, 'but I don't think you should go. I don't think you are at all suited to my son or he to you. I really don't.'

'Oh, be quiet, Mother,' Rupert cried irritably.

'Don't you dare tell me to be quiet,' Gladys echoed Selina firmly and Rupert grimaced

118

between the two women. This was not at all the way it should be. In his father's world the women did what you told them, but here he was being ordered about all over the place like a recalcitrant schoolboy. How dare they criticise him!

Daniella sat down again and Carlo began to organise the dinner party into some semblance of order. The waiters hovered. The *maître d'* allowed his disapproval of the crowded table to show, but not at the expense of courtesy and efficiency.

Marcello, under Ariana's hawk-like scrutiny, was whispering urgently to Daniella, 'I've got to talk to you alone,' and when Gladys, perusing a huge menu, looked around the table and announced, 'Rupert is all wrong for Dani. I always knew it. No, my son, Selina is the girl for you, believe me. But I reckon you're too stupid to see it.'

And Selina glanced around the table with wide-eyed innocence as if to say, who me? then burst out laughing. Her laughter was infectious and soon everyone had joined her except Rupert who scowled morosely and glared fixedly at the chandelier.

119

CHAPTER SEVENTEEN

The moon spilled over the Roman roofs, silvering them so that the city looked enchanted. Daniella could see the ancient outline of the Colosseum as they drove around it in silence. There were shadows dancing through the porticos and she wondered if the ghosts of old decadent emperors wandered in and out with the cats, unable to find peace, or whether the wraiths that haunted the echoing ruin were the spirits of the victims who died there so horribly, yet so bravely. How small her problems seemed compared to the events that huge edifice had witnessed; the gore, the violent deaths against a background of thousands. What was happening to her was, comparatively speaking, minor, yet it hurt. Everything was relative.

Marcello drove the car towards the villa with competent speed. He was silent.

Ariana and Carlo had manipulated the conversation through the minefield of Gladys's periodic frank observations. Daniella was grateful for their tact and dexterity. Selina had assured them all that her presence was purely supportive. Rupert, she informed them, was nervous of flying.

'He's not had any experience,' Gladys said.

'He's green,' Selina commented, relishing

120

the word, repeated it again. 'Green.'

Which observation Rupert denied vehemently, only to have his mother cry, 'Why of course you, are, son,' and to his mortification she informed the rest of the table, 'Rupert's almost never been out of the country in his life. His father insisted his plane would crash.' She winked at her son, 'Wrong again there, wasn't he, Rupert? His father told us the food would poison us. Or he'd be set about by brigands in "foreign parts", as he called anywhere outside England. Everyone except his fellow-countrymen were barbarians, he told us. I always wanted to ask him what he thought the football hooligans were, but I never had the courage.'

'You came to Italy for your honeymoon, didn't you, Rupert?' Ariana asked kindly, trying to save the situation, keep the peace.

'For twenty-four hours!' Daniella could not resist remarking. 'You were in Italy twenty-four hours. Then he insisted we return to London.'

'I know how you feel though,' Ariana interpolated swiftly. 'Sometimes I think, when we're crossing the Atlantic, say, what on earth am I doing up here, in this little tin can, buffeted by wind and at the mercy of the elements.'

'If God had meant us to fly he'd have given us wings,' Gladys announced. 'That's what my Henry used to say. He did in a way, didn't He

121

though? God. He gave us the men who invented the wings. Marconi or somebody . . .'

'The Wright brothers,' Carlo supplied gently.

'Oh! Yes, well, it was my first flight. Henry said all sorts of dire things would happen and all that did was I had a lovely chat with Selina. It wasn't so different to getting the fifty-two bus.' She grinned around the table. 'I think it's terribly exciting. Better than mules and donkeys. And,' she added, peering around at them through the curtain of her mascara, 'think of the *Titanic*!'

'I'm feeling a bit . . .' Daniella half rose and Marcello swiftly took her arm.

'I'll take you home,' he said in a very deliberate voice.

'You'll do no such thing,' Rupert protested, hurrying around the table to his wife.

'I think you better let Marcello drive her, Rupert,' Ariana said firmly. 'He's got his car and you have no transport.'

Rupert hesitated and Marcello steered Daniella to the entrance.

Daniella let herself be led. She felt as if she was participating in some sort of weird play where everyone did and said the exact opposite of what she expected. A bit like Alice in Wonderland.

Just before they left the table, Carlo said he'd do the honours but Ariana pulled him back down, whispering fiercely, 'Go, go,

Marcello! Sit, Carlo. Do.' And Ariana waved her hands as if shooing them out of the restaurant.

So Daniella had no option but to go with Marcello and now sat quietly beside him as he drove through the moonlit city.

The ball of hysteria she had felt inside her in the Excelsior had melted and disappeared as he drove. The warm shadows of the night relaxed her and she felt suddenly safe in the car with him the cool night air on her cheeks. He allowed her time, was quiet beside her, his presence reassuring.

When they reached the villa she instantly made as if to jump out of the car, grappling with the door handle. He put a gentle restraining hand on her arm.

'Why do you treat me like this? As if I were a monster?' he asked softly. Embarrassed she stopped pulling at the handle.

'Oh I don't mean to. It's just ... so complicated.'

'For me it is not,' he said, and putting his hands on her shoulders he turned her gently towards him. 'Look, I think I love you,' he said, then shook his head, 'No. No, I *do* love you. There's no doubt about it. I can't stop thinking about you, Daniella. You are in my heart all the time. Everywhere I go I see your little face. You haunt me.' He shook his head. 'There, you see. I promised myself I wouldn't say these silly things to you, these clichés, but,' he shrugged, 'they are all true. I fell in love with you when you tripped me up with your bag-strap in the hotel and I saw your beautiful sad little face for the first time. I wanted to mend you. To make you laugh. Make you happy.'

She was looking at him breathlessly. She yearned for him to continue but something held her back. Fear. He was just saying this because she had flown from him. Men hated rejection, even she knew that. The best way to keep a man's interest was to run away. Was he just intent on conquest? How could she trust him when her experience was so limited?

'Oh Marcello, please. It's all too . . .'

'You feel something for me?' he asked eagerly. 'Return some . . . something? The other night must have meant something to you.'

'Oh yes,' she breathed. 'Oh yes. But you've seen . . . tonight . . . My husband. It is too soon . . .'

He stared at her in the moonlight, then drew her gently into his arms and was kissing her ardently. She lay passive in his embrace but gradually she began to return his kisses. They were gentle yet passionate and once more she was aware how completely different he was to Rupert. How different the taste of him, the feel of him, how very different her response.

'I love you, *cara mia*, very much. And I will

124

wait patiently for you, but please don't cut me out. Don't run away.'

'I won't,' she promised.

They looked at each other a long moment and then she nodded. 'Oh, don't think me silly, Marcello, but I feel at home in your arms, as if it was right. The right place for me to be,' she said softly.

'Then, don't you see? We were meant for each other. This was meant to happen.' His exuberance bubbled over, alarmed her.

'Give me a little more time,' she pleaded.

'Of course,' he replied, smiling at her. 'Forgive me. I thought, you see, that this would never happen to me, so I am, how you say? Precipitate? You are worth waiting for,' he told her.

'There is a hard, cold little knot inside me, Marcello, that stops me from being spontaneous. Of giving . . . not my body but my heart.'

'And it is your heart I want most.' Then he laughed and rolled his eyes. 'Of course I want your body too. I would be mad not to,' then seriously again, 'But, *cara*, it is your heart I am after.'

She kissed him, leaning forward as she had done that first time. She could feel the cold centre of her being dissolve a little more each time he touched her.

'Thank you,' she whispered, got out of the car and was inside the house before he could pull himself together. He sighed and smiling to himself drove away.

CHAPTER EIGHTEEN

'He's run away again! Rupert's pissed off and left me holding the can,' Selina announced next morning.

Daniella had risen early to find her sister with Maria in the kitchen squeezing oranges. The room opened onto the terrace and the table there, under its blue and white striped umbrella, was laid out for breakfast. The glasses were blue Venetian and the napkins and tablecloth an exquisite blue and white design. There was a huge bowl of fruit and fresh bread from the bakery in a covered basket.

'You got home all right then?' Ariana asked slyly, glancing at Daniella's radiant face. Daniella had been in bed when the party returned from the Excelsior. She stared a moment at her sister then winked at her. 'Ah yes! I see!'

'No, you don't,' Daniella blushed. It was all so new to her and she was acutely aware how unsophisticated she was.

'Then tell me. You owe me,' Ariana insisted. 'I have opened my house to your husband, his mother and his girlfriend . . .'

'She's *not* his girlfriend,' Daniella protested, wondering why that bothered her. Ariana laughed.

'No matter what you say *I* think she's going to be his girlfriend. If he's any sense at all . . .'

'Which I doubt . . .'

'He'll grab her *tout de suite*, as she's so fond of saying. Actually, I think she's fun.'

'They're here? You've really got them here? Rupert . . .' Daniella looked about nervously.

'Yes. They're here.' Ariana handed her sister a blue glass full of orange juice.

'Here? In the villa?' Why was she so nervous? Angrily she tried to control her apprehension.

'Um, yes. They're all here. Look Dani, don't worry, please. Rupert has no power over you any more. Just you remember that,' Ariana was saying.

'How come?' Daniella asked her. 'You must be nuts, Ari. You must not be imposed on like that. It's not fair.'

'Oh, it's rather fun. I'm enjoying it.'

'My life is in ruins and you're *enjoying* it? What, was Rupert hassling you? Did he insist . . .'

'No, Dani. I offered. They'd come here directly from the airport and Maria told them where we were so they went straight to the restaurant. I couldn't let them traipse around Rome looking for a hotel at that time of night . . .'

'You stayed . . .'

'Another hour at least after you'd gone. Gladys was very . . .' Ariana searched for the right word, ' . . . entertaining. She also got a bit drunk.'

'Good God, no! I've never seen her touch alcohol.' Daniella felt her heart sink. She felt vulnerable and exposed. Her husband and his family seemed intent on making nuisances of themselves and turning what was, to her, a powerful confusion mixed with a tremendous dawning of love and joy, into turmoil.

Ariana led her onto the terrace and seated her firmly at the table.

'She doesn't drink, Ari. Didn't drink. Oh, I'm so sorry, the world has gone mad.' Daniella looked distracted as she drank her juice.

All the shadows were now gone except for the shade under the eucalyptus tree. The sun shone butter-yellow and there was the whisper of a sweet-scented breeze. Around the terrace the bougainvillaea was a gaudy splash of cerise and the wisteria draped its delicate mauve bunches artistically around the lattice overhead.

'Henry, her husband, has had a stroke,' Ariana was saying, 'and apparently she's parked him in a nursing home and she refuses to have him at home. She hasn't a good word to say about him.'

Daniella stuck her pale legs out from under

the umbrella into the sun. 'How grim!'

Ariana stared out over the roofs of the city. 'How badly he must have treated her to generate such total rejection,' she said.

'Like father, like son. Which I suppose means that if I'd stayed with Rupert I'd be like her.'

Ariana laughed. 'Oh, she's not so bad,' she said. 'In fact I like her. I think she's making up for lost time.'

'Umm,' Daniella grunted, her mind elsewhere.

'They came back with us last night. I knocked on your door but you didn't answer. So I thought you might have company,' she added slyly.

Daniella turned her head away. 'No. I was asleep. Anyhow I wouldn't do that. Not in your home. It would be an imposition.' Daniella turned around and faced her sister. She took a roll from under the napkin in the basket and tore it apart.

'Well, come on,' Ariana cried. 'Tell all. You can't fool me, Dani, so spill the beans. You haven't told me everything, have you? You've been secretive and . . . and sly, which is not like you.'

'Because I'm frightened and shy and I don't know what I'm doing,' she said. 'That's why I haven't told you everything.'

'Seems to me you've been doing all right. Just fine.' Then seeing her sister's face full of anguish she was immediately contrite and pulling her chair near her sister's she put her arms around the distressed girl.

'Come on, Dani, don't be afraid. Just tell your big sister what's up.'

Daniella confided then, all that had happened since her arrival in Rome. Ariana listened with great attention, looking up only once when the sound of a car at the front of the house distracted her.

'It must be Carlo,' she remarked. 'He's off to work.'

'But don't you want to say goodbye . . .'

'No. He'll have realised that we're having a heart to heart.' She grinned at her sister, 'I brought him breakfast in bed earlier.' Then she leaned forward again, 'Go on, go on. This is fascinating.'

Daniella tried to be completely honest and give her sister a clear picture of events.

'He says he loves me, Ari. He sounded so sincere, but how am I to know? He was awfully hurt when I sent him packing . . .'

'You really did that? Why?'

'I was so scared. I felt I'd betrayed Rupert.' Ariana snorted. 'And I felt I'd been, oh, I don't know, I'd cheapened myself.'

'Absolutely not. Oh Dani, Marcello is that rare thing, a lovely man. He's kind and sincere and if he says he loves you I'd bet my bottom dollar he means it. Besides,' she looked her sister straight in the eye, 'you'll have to learn

130

to trust, you really will. You'll have to learn to take risks.'

They talked until Selina arrived on the terrace with the news that Rupert had done a bunk. It turned out that Carlo had had a passenger travelling with him to the city and then by taxi to the airport.

'He's gone? Are you sure?' Ariana asked and Daniella felt a surge of relief. Selina nodded. She was wearing a silk kimono and looked to Daniella disgustingly beautiful.

'His room's empty. No, he's gone with the wind. Didn't even say goodbye.' She looked at Daniella. 'How'd you stand it, these years, with him not even house-broken? Very bad show.'

She didn't wait for a reply but looked out at the warm morning view over Rome and stretched and shook her hair. 'Oh my God, it's heaven here,' she cried. 'Absolute bliss.' Then she looked at Ariana. 'You're frightfully kind, you really are. Welcoming total strangers into your home.'

Ariana smiled. 'Oh, Rupert is not, unfortunately, a total stranger. I've only laid eyes on his mum twice in my life and she's changed so much since I last saw her, she might as well be a stranger. *You* are the only *total* stranger and you are very welcome indeed. Especially,' she glanced at her sister, 'if you can take Rupert off our hands.'

'If Daniella's quite sure she's finished with him?' Selina raised an eyebrow quizically.

'Sure am,' Daniella said. 'Though why you'd want him I simply cannot think.'

'Challenge! I want to have a go. House-train him.'

Daniella looked at her incredulously. 'You can't be serious.'

'Your problem, Daniella, is you let him walk all over you. No one walks over me, believe me. I've just recently walloped him in court, had him at my mercy in the airport,' she giggled, 'trying to pretend he was being a gentleman, giving me precedence when all the time it was obvious he was inept, didn't know what to do, where to go. I've seen him totally routed by you, his wife, walking out on him, the one person he believed he could boss and bully. And then, his mother! Apparently she's done a volte-face, the worm turns, that sort of thing.' Daniella nodded. 'He's a mess. But I'll pick him up, dust him down and put him together again. To *my* satisfaction. Unlike the King's horses and the King's men I'll be able to put Humpty-Dumpty together again.'

'Bravo! Bravo!' The clapping came from Gladys, who emerged onto the terrace shading her eyes with her hand. 'Oh God, I feel ghastly,' she said, blinking rapidly in the sunshine. 'But happy. I'm sick as a parrot but I'm a very joyful parrot, a contented bird who just happens to have a terrible headache.' She sat down at the breakfast table. 'That was the best evening of my life,' she announced.

132

'Ballistic, as the youngsters say.'

'Your mother-in-law was flirting outrageously with a young waiter,' Ariana told Daniella.

'I had a ball,' Gladys sighed.

'I'll get you some Alka-Seltzer,' Ariana told her but Gladys shook her head.

'No, no,' she cried, wincing painfully, 'I'll nurse it a bit longer. It reminds me, you see, that I've been out there, partying, doing it, not criticising everyone who was having a good time, but having a good time myself. No, I'll hang onto this *agony* a wee bit longer, thank you.'

Ariana laughed and they sat drinking *caffé latte*, eating rolls and casually chatting in the warm Italian morning.

CHAPTER NINETEEN

The room was high-ceilinged, formal, with huge gilt mirrors on the walls and ancient portraits. The furniture was Empire. There was a fire in the enormous grate even though the temperature outside was in the eighties. It burned lazily, smouldering sulkily and shooting off meteoric sparks every now and then.

The little lady sitting there, back stiff as a ramrod, priceless pink pearls heavy around her neck stared into the fire, a small frown the

133

only sign of emotion on her face.

Her son, her heir, had broken the habit of years and had fallen in love. Worse, he had fallen for a married woman. An Englishwoman. Oh sure, she had Italian blood, but not Italian upbringing. She was the daughter of tradespeople. Not of their society, not of their *milieu*.

Katerina Vestori had grown complacent. She had decided that Bella was sufficient for her son's needs and perhaps her beloved Marcello would remain entirely hers.

They had always been close, but—and she hated to admit this—Marcello was an indifferent businessman. At least on the administration side. On the management side he proved far too *nice* to be really successful. Her daughter Antoinella's husband, Christano, now he, he was a shark. Antoinella was Signora Vestori's daughter and she and her husband were far more capable of running the family business than Marcello, who would always allow his good manners and sweet nature to give in to their competitors. He would overlook a disadvantage in case he upset somebody.

No, her beloved son was a terrific salesman but nothing more. If she gave him an executive post he'd have the most elite shoe company in the world ruined in less time than it would take to bless himself. She was sad to have to admit that but it was true. And Katerina was a realist.

But Marcello did not mind. He was such a delightful young man and until now, except for the fact that he was incapable of running the Vestori business, he had been the perfect son.

But, it appeared, all that was about to change.

So, Signora Katerina Vestori had done the only thing she could think of: she had sent for Bella.

The courtesan had been flown from Rome to Pisa at her request in the private Vestori jet and was on her way now to the house on the Via Della Spada. The house was high-walled, a courtyard leading to the entrance. Kalo, the chauffeur had called on the mobile from the company limo to say that they were even now on their way. All this after Marcello had phoned the startling news from Rome that he had met someone special and had, at last, fallen in love.

The flurry of activity was intense but efficient. Katerina sighed. She was sorry she was going to have to break this woman's heart. She had nothing personal against Daniella Weston. She sounded like a nice girl. But she was a married woman so it was impossible. In an old Catholic family like the Vestoris the *status quo* had to be preserved and divorce was unacceptable. Daniella would divorce her husband, certainly, but Marcello could not marry a divorced woman, no matter what the

Grimaldis did. She tut-tutted to herself. That family in Monaco had done immeasurable harm to the Holy Roman Catholic Church, manipulating the Vatican to suit their purposes. Katerina shook her head in disgust. That, she told herself, was what happened when you allowed foreigners and film stars to infiltrate the old families. No, this Daniella Weston would have to go.

There was a knock on the door and her personal maid, Angelica, grown old in her service, entered without waiting for a reply, bearing a silver tray of exquisite craftsmanship laden with a silver pot of coffee, cups and a Chinese tea-pot containing a *tisane*. Much to Katerina's regret her ageing stomach could not manage coffee any more but she had asked for coffee in case her visitor desired it. There were *amoretti* in a cut-glass dish and pink and white sugar almonds. Little silver containers with cream and sugar crowded against the fine china.

'Put it there, Anjelica,' she commanded, unnecessarily, for Anjelica knew very well where to put the tray, having done so every day at this time for the last thirty years.

'Show the . . . lady up when she arrives,' she told the servant as she was leaving the room. Then Katerina returned to her reflections.

She liked things as they were. It suited her that her cut-throat son-in-law was the prime mover and shaker in the Vestori empire. He had single-handedly dragged the shoe company screaming and kicking into the modern market. If Christano got too big for his boots she could always get rid of him, and he knew that. It was something she could never do to Marcello, her son. Christano was not a Vestori, after all. He was expendable no matter what Antoinella thought.

No, it worried her not at all that Marcello was not the leader of commerce that she had once hoped he would be. Instead she had him around, enjoyed his charming company without the inevitable tension business partners generated. She had been very content with the situation *vis-á-vis* his love life. She preferred to call it that to 'sex life', which she was old enough to find faintly shocking. A tiny bit crude.

Bella was a delightful and discreet mistress, a perfect arrangement for someone like Marcello and as Katerina had no ambitions for Marcello to produce an heir the arrangement suited her very well.

Antoinella had already given her grandchildren and little Leonardo and Donato were waiting in the wings to take centre-stage when they reached the appropriate age. And when the shark decided to give the power, which Katerina knew would not be for a very long time indeed.

Signora Vestori was a woman who enjoyed her life as it was, and she did not want things to change. Marcello escorted her to the opera, they had regular lunches and dinner together. He lived here with her in the house in Florence and she was always aware of his presence even when he was in and out and their paths did not cross. His presence about the place made her happy. She liked him joining her for meals in the long cool dining room and when he was in town she savoured their amusing conversations, for Marcello was that rare creature, the perfect companion, attentive to her moods, intuitive and entertaining.

She poured the vervain tea and as she sipped it there was a gentle tap on the door and Bella made her entrance.

'*Buona sera, Signora,*' Bella greeted the older woman. '*Come sta?*'

'I am well, *grazie*. Or as well as someone my age ever is.'

'*Signora*! You look amazing. One would never believe you were a grandmother.'

The niceties meticulously observed, Katrina indicated a chair opposite her and Bella sat down.

She was modestly dressed. She had been careful not to look obtrusive in her pale silk dress and coat to match. She had a very good idea why the matriarch had sent for her, and Bella, knowing where her good fortune lay, was composed and ready for the older woman's suggestions.

'This is a delicate matter,' Katerina began.

'*Si, Signora*. Anything you say, I assure you of my discretion.'

'Yes. Well. No need to play hide and seek, eh? I know of, *have* known of your, er, *liaison* with my son . . .'

'Signora, I assure you . . .'

'Stop saying that! I am not a fool. I know you are the soul of tact. I am aware how diplomatic you have been in your dealings with my son.' She regarded the woman opposite her with critical scrutiny.

She was indeed beautiful, a voluptuous woman in the full blooming of her sexual charms. Her skin was ripe as an apricot, invited caresses. And her body, curving like a Matisse nude, begged to be embraced. Katerina sighed. Once she too had been desirable and, although she had always been slim as a lily-stem and lacked the opulence of the woman opposite her, men had queued up to court her.

'As I said, the matter is delicate.' She cleared her throat and Bella waited patiently, wishing she'd get to the point and that the chair was more comfortable.

'My son has been, it appears, *consorting* with a married English lady.' Bella at once grasped the formidable lady's drift. She wanted to summarise the older woman's rambling and cut to the chase: 'I get it. You don't want him to be with Daniella Weston and you want me

139

to break it up.' But she said nothing and allowed the matriarch to witter on and endlessly on.

The thought disgusted her. To send a mistress in to break someone's heart did not seem fair to her, but then, Bella knew full well how little others' feelings meant to the powerful when intent on getting what they wanted. She listened, gazing raptly at Signora Vestori, and waited. It eventually emerged from a vast amount of verbiage exactly as Bella anticipated.

Signora Vestori announced point-blank, 'I will not have a Vestori marry a divorcée and that is that. We are an ancient Catholic family and it simply will not do. I will have to find a nice pretty young Italian Catholic girl for him, preferably a girl from Florence. But not this woman. I want you to go to Positano where I hear they are and put an end to this misalliance. Kalo will fly you to Naples and your hotel expenses will all be taken care of. I have given Kalo a cheque to cover any requirements you may have. Meals et cetera, and some new pretty clothes. You may wish to take a companion. I leave it to you.'

Bella was not proud. She was greedy. Her upbringing had made her very insecure about money; there was not enough of it ever to make her feel secure.

She needed a little break. A little escape to the sea, out of the city, so it all fitted nicely.

They exchanged pleasantries in a desultory fashion but Bella could see that for Signora Vestori the interview was over and she was impatient for Bella to go.

'*Buona sera, Signora.*' She rose to her feet and the old woman waved her hand in grand dismissal. Bella left the woman alone in front of the fire, rubbing her hands together as if she were very cold.

CHAPTER TWENTY

Rupert was extremely cross. Bloody women! They had ganged up on him, all of them ranged against him, made him feel small, laughed at his weaknesses and condemned him for what his father had told him was the best way to handle the opposite sex and love and marriage. It simply was not fair. Was his father totally misguided, and if so what the devil was Rupert supposed to do, how to behave? He had to admit he hadn't a clue and that made him feel helpless and angry.

He thundered through the airport, onto the plane and back to London, more sure of the technicalities and rituals this time, and arrived home to a chill, dusty and utterly unkempt house. Empty of food, of comfort, of tidiness, of company. Of all the things he had been assured by his father a woman was supposed to supply. He sat down in the living room, dejected, and nearly wept.

Why had this happened to him? Where had he gone wrong? He shivered sitting there in the gloom, his holdall at his feet. He felt lonely and deserted and there seemed to be no one he could turn to.

He left the house and went to the top of the road. He bought some French bread from the patisserie on Holland Park Avenue, along with cheese, wine, black olives from Provence and freshly ground Colombian coffee.

As he left the delicatessen a group of Arab women, draped in black, only their eyes visible, shrouded in mystery, passed him by slowly, carrying their layers of fat with sensuous confidence. Now that's how women should be, Rupert thought. Half the world thinks that is their proper place, under veils, under wraps, their men's property. Yet, a small voice within him protested, why is it that the woman most on my mind is the stroppiest, the most contentious, the absolutely independent Selina Wright? He shook his head in bewilderment and went back to the house.

He felt a good deal better when he'd opened the shutters, brewed the coffee and was munching the crusty bread, savouring the cheese and olives, but still the question persisted: where had he gone wrong?

He mused in a more detached frame of mind. When you came right down to it (and

Rupert was reluctant to admit it), it seemed to him that there was no one to blame for absolutely everything but himself and his father. Well, he amended virtuously, mainly his father.

He'd idolised the man, believed everything he'd told him; but his father, it appeared, had been wrong, wrong, wrong. Unless you happened to live in Abu Dhabi.

The biggest shock of all was the discovery that his mother had been unhappy all these years. How was he to have known that? As a boy, growing up, he'd have sworn they were a contented household, a devoted family. His mother always smiling, bustling about, doing, as he thought then, her rightful job, looking after men. Cooking, cleaning, washing and ironing. His father often said, 'It's a privilege, Rupert. There is nothing more satisfying for a wife and mother than being busy in the kitchen, looking after her men. Isn't that right, Gladys?' And his mother would nod and smile and murmur, 'Oh yes, Henry dear, yes.'

How could he have guessed she was lying? Even now he couldn't quite credit it. Perhaps she didn't want to look after her husband and was making up all this about being unhappy. And then listening to his father pontificating about things, how could Rupert know that the father he revered was, in fact, hopelessly misguided and Victorian in his attitudes and beliefs. That much Rupert had become aware

143

of.

Rupert watched some television before he went to bed, looking with new eyes and insight at the underlying messages the soaps, the news, all the programmes carried, and it came to him that they were all without exception indicating that his mother, his wife, her sister and most of all Selina Wright were correct and that his father had been wrong.

It appeared that if he wanted to have a happy relationship, any happy relationship, he'd have to change radically. Re-think his beliefs. Reverse them. Learn to do the opposite of what he had hitherto believed was right.

As it happened, the story of that evening's episode of *The Bill* was all about a bullying husband and Rupert winced listening to this man as he shouted at his intimidated wife, yelling, his face red, putting her down just as he had done Dani. He could see that everyone in the programme despised this man. The police made remarks deploring his behaviour, the neighbours shook their heads and called him a bully. And the female cops were disgusted with him. Why hadn't he noticed this before? How could he have been so blind?

Rupert slept uneasily that night, haunted by the red-faced bully on '*The Bill*'. Then in his dreams the bully's face suddenly changed into his own and the cowed wife became Daniella and in his sleep he cringed, buried himself low in the bed, burrowing down deeper as if he was crawling into a hole, or back into the womb.

He was awakened by the shrilling of the telephone. Fighting the bedclothes and pillows he struggled up and, uncovering his head, groped for the receiver.

'Hi, Rupe,' the voice light and bright. Selina. He groaned inwardly.

'Hello Selina,' he replied, 'Where are you?'

'Rome, you idiot. With your sister-in-law. Why the hell did you desert me?' She sounded angry now.

'Well, I . . .'

'Oh, cut it out, Rupe. It's not on, really it's not. You beg me to leave everything and go with you to Italy—'

'But you were on leave so—'

'Don't you *dare* say it didn't matter. My leave is precious to me, you selfish bastard. You dump me on your poor sister-in-law and your wife, you desert me in the middle of nowhere—'

'Oh, come now, Selina, Ariana's is not in the middle of nowhere—'

'Don't you interrupt me when I'm talking, Rupe. Where are your manners? For your information, in my book Ariana's house *is* the middle of nowhere. You're so god-damn selfish you haven't realised that I've no car. And when I hire one you'll foot the bill, don't worry. I'm cooped up here with your mother who is quite potty—'

145

'Selina! My mother is not—'

'Not another word! As I said, with your potty mother, your delightful sister-in-law who does not know me from Adam and on whom I have imposed long enough. And as I've said, I've no transport. Daniella, by the way, like the swallows in winter, has flown with Marcello southward. To Naples, I think. Or somewhere near there. Amalfi. Positano.'

'Positano . . .' He winced, thinking instantly of their honeymoon. 'No, she couldn't! She wouldn't!'

'I heard her say. She said, by the way, that if I saw you to tell you *not* to follow her. She said this Marcello is absolutely wonderful, that she loves him—'

'She can't! Don't be daft. They've only just met.'

'Rupert, Rupert, I despair of you. How long did it take Romeo? Don't you see? Daniella was like a caged bird desperate to fly. You kept her caged but she's flying now and whether or not this Marcello is the right man for her is beside the point. The thing is, she's found her feet. She's freed herself from captivity and slavery and she's gone where you can't reach her. And I don't just mean her location.'

There was silence. 'Are you there, Rupe? Aren't you going to give me an argument?' The silence continued, then Rupert's voice, subdued.

'Well, no. You're probably right.'

146

'Say that again.'

'I said, you're probably right.'

'Good grief! I doubted my ears just now. So listen, my lord and master,' she sounded sarcastic, 'what are my instructions? I feel as if I've failed you, although I never promised you results *and* I have to say, if you must know, I believe everything has turned out for the best.'

'Yes. I think so too.'

'What?' she squeaked. 'Do you? Really, Rupe?'

'Yes.'

'Well then, that's that! I'll pack my bag and return to dear old London . . .' But he stopped her.

'No, no. I have a better idea. It's awful here . . .'

'Without the slave . . .'

'Why don't you stay there?' he suggested. 'After all, you're on holiday and I've taken time off. I'll come back to Rome . . .'

'It's getting hot here . . .'

'We'll go south. Find out where Dani is—'

'Oh no!'

'—and go *elsewhere.*'

'You're sure you're not . . . She was very insistent you shouldn't . . .'

'No, no. I don't *want* to see her. Not really.'

'All right then. I'll wait here with Ariana till you get back.' A pause then she cried, 'Good Lord, Rupe, you have changed. Two flights, no, *three* within a week . . . Good grief, you'll

147

be a jetsetter in no time at all.' There was silence at the other end and she said, 'Rupe? Rupe, you there?'

'Selina, will you help me? I mean with . . . everything?'

'I know what you mean and I'm only too pleased,' she laughed. 'Don't worry, Rupe, I'll make a man of you yet.'

CHAPTER TWENTY-ONE

Ariana fingered Carla's curls, the soft little tendrils of golden hair at the nape of her neck. They were home from school and the evening was drawing in, the sky over Rome a salmon pink. Ariana and Selina were drinking tea.

'This guy then, this Marcello, he okay?' Selina asked, looking across the terrace to where her hostess sat with her children.

Paola stood by her mother fingering Ariana's hair in the exact same manner as her mother played with Carla's curls. She's copying her mother, Selina thought, but also reflected that there was something sad in the child's copy-cat actions.

They had been like that for a long time when Selina, who had been watching the shadows slide down behind the spires and domes of the city, glanced back at the little group and saw Ariana irritably shake her daughter's fingers away. She watched as Paola let go of her hair instantly. For a moment she looked as if she might cry, then she shoved Carla off her mother's lap quite viciously. The little girl yelled angrily and in her turn pushed Paola who, off-balance, fell on the floor. They rolled around together pushing and shoving but, Selina could see, restraining themselves nevertheless. If they were boys there would be no restraint, she decided, and Ariana cried:

'Stop it, girls, stop it at once!' And both little girls burst into loud weeping and wailing.

'Go into the playroom at once and stop that caterwauling. Maria,' she called. 'Maria!' and when the servant appeared, 'Take them inside, Maria, they are being naughty. Very naughty.'

When they had gone she looked back at her guest.

'You were asking about Marcello. Well,' she rolled her eyes, 'he's delightful. Daniella could not have chosen better. He's a lovely man, unmarried . . .'

'Why?'

'Well, he's not gay, if that's what you mean.'

'One has to ask.'

'He has a mistress. Very beautiful. For years if what they say is true.'

'Will he tell Daniella?'

Ariana stared at her as if she was crazy. 'Are you mad? Of course not. Why should he? It's not her business.'

'I'd want to know,' Selina said, sipping her

tea. 'I'd wonder why so handsome and urbane a man had never been married and I'd ferret it out.'

'And what would you gain? A thousand doubts and questions and uncertainties. Anyway, Daniella's not like you, Selina. She's not at all sophisticated. She's blindly happy with this man. She's no ability to analyse, to query. She is quite simply madly in love,' she glanced at Selina, 'and you know, I do believe, so is Marcello.'

'Well, I think that's great,' Selina said thoughtfully. Then, as Ariana put down her cup and lit a cigarette, she asked, 'What did you mean when you said Daniella was not like me? Do you think I'm hard?'

Ariana laughed, 'So you *do* care what people think of you! Oh no. Of course not hard. But you like to pretend you are.'

'Actually, I am hard,' Selina murmured gloomily. 'Oh dear, how awful!'

'No, my dear, you are not hard. You are confident, incisive, you know what you want and you are not afraid to go after it. That's not being hard. If you were hard you'd not bother with that question, would you? You wouldn't care one way or the other.' Ariana glanced at her quizzically. 'And as a matter of interest, why aren't you married?'

Selina shrugged. 'I suppose because I have a sort of love-hate relationship with the opposite sex. You see, I believe all men are really fools.'

To her surprise Ariana nodded in agreement. 'Sure they are, but such sweet fools. You can't blame them for that.'

'I can,' Selina smiled.

' . . . and we need them. Well,' she amended, 'I need Carlo. I love him. He is good for me. Not like Rupert and Daniella.'

'Men make war. They are violent. Look at history, Ariana. Look at football matches . . .'

'Oh, I'd rather not.' Ariana was amused at the girl's intensity.

'Do you see women in their hundreds marching to war? Never. We'd try to find a solution. We'd sit down and talk. You don't find gangs of females beating up old women, raping them.' She shook her heavy mane of hair. 'Oh, we get it in the courts all the time. Sniggering, primitive yobbos, chaps who clobber old dears and violate them for a fiver, a tenner. Destroy their peace forever. Unspeakably foul crimes, rarely perpetuated by females.' She glanced at Ariana. 'I'm not suggesting for a moment that we are all saints, whiter than white. Not for a moment. Women can be vindictive evil, commit murder . . . look at Rosemary West and Myra Hindley. You don't get worse than that. But, *but*,' she wagged a finger, 'you do *not* see us in gangs, fighting at football matches, outside pubs, marching down roads in Belfast, goose-stepping in their hundreds and thousands in Iran and Iraq. Parading the streets of Germany

151

in wave after wave with Nazi slogans and swastikas tattooed all over us. *And*, talking of that, it was mainly men, and I am not saying exclusively but mostly, who comprised Hitler's army, who sacked Rome, who invaded Poland, went over the hill at Gallipoli, who annihilated the peoples of South America and who nearly wiped out the Indians in the north, who persecute, occupy, terrorise and subjugate or try to, nations, countries, societies and homes. There! That's my position.'

Ariana nodded and laughed, holding up her hands as if to halt the flow. 'Okay, okay. And sometimes you'll have to concede they had to do it for a good purpose.'

Selina shook her head. 'No. They must have been able to talk—'

Ariana interrupted her, 'Yet if you so passionately believe this, why of all the men in the world did you choose Rupert Weston?'

'What makes you think I've chosen him?'

'Oh, come on, Selina. It's obvious.'

Selina thought a moment, then she said, 'I don't honestly know.' She screwed up her eyes, thinking, as a purple twilight shimmered over the city and Maria came out and lit the mosquito repellent candles. 'I think maybe he epitomises everything I despise, the arrogance, the sexism, the bullying tactics and yet I believe I can change that.'

'A female Professor Higgins?'

'Oh, much worthier. He changed an accent

and manners. I'm trying to change cruelty and closed-mindedness.'

'Do you think you'll succeed?'

'I don't know, Ariana. But I believe that with Rupert, as with a lot of men, it is only skin-deep, all a façade. If they could stop worrying about their macho image, about what people thought of them.' She shrugged. 'I don't know. But I think that underneath he is a frightened child who has never been trained. And maybe, just maybe, *I* could train him.' She grinned at Ariana. 'Oh, I know what you'll say. That I'm the perennial woman trying to change her man. I know I couldn't, wouldn't even try with a man whose beliefs were firmly entrenched, but you've got to remember that Daniella left him, which has bewildered him and confused him . . .'

'And his almighty father has had a stroke, for believe me he wouldn't have come here if old man Weston had been able to issue orders.'

'And his mother has had a metamorphosis which has alarmed hell out of him.'

'And he found Daniella with someone else. Realised that she found someone else desirable.'

'And he lost a very important case in front of the whole legal world in London.'

'Making a complete twit of himself . . .'

'This man, Ariana, has been put through the wringer and is, shall we say, clay in my hands.'

Ariana grunted. 'I'm not that happy about him coming here,' she admitted. 'I've never liked him and I resent terribly what he did to my sister and how he behaved when he was here before.'

'Don't worry, Ariana. As soon as he arrives I'll pile him into the Hertz I've rented and we'll take off for the South. Anywhere but where Daniella is.' She glanced at Ariana. 'Where is she, by the way? I need to know so we don't clash.'

'She and Marcello are in Positano in Papa's friend's hotel. The one she went to on her honeymoon.'

Selina whistled. 'Wow! Was that wise?'

'Aparently, and according to her it has laid to rest all sorts of horrible memories. I spoke to her this morning and she was ecstatic.'

'Okay. Then we'll skip Positano. We'll make for Sorrento and I'll wrangle him into shape, see if I don't. You won't know him when I've done with him.'

Ariana looked doubtful. 'Is he really worth it, Selina?' she asked, and Selina, rising from her chair, stretched and looked out over the city below, at the stars dancing about and the moon silvering the world in a shimmering cloak.

'You bet,' she said. 'You bet.'

CHAPTER TWENTY-TWO

Gladys, in one of her saner moments, had phoned the bank and credit-card company allied to it and discovered to her astonished delight that she was a rich woman. Her husband, being a careful and parsimonious man, had been ultra-cautious with their money over the years and their credit account showed a considerable balance, while their saving account and the stocks and shares which were in this day and age as gilt-edged as it was possible to be, revealed a breathtakingly large nest-egg that she had not known existed. The interest alone would support her in a style to which she was not at all accustomed, a luxurious way of life she was eager to embrace and which she had never dreamed possible. It also ensured that she could make sure that Henry would be taken care of. In the twilight zone he found himself in Gladys could ensure that he had the best possible care twenty-four hours a day. And she could forget about him.

The thought of him, however, was ever present. Deep down in the depths of her mind, well below the surface, a little voice carried on a running commentary, a diatribe slating their life together.

'You know you made me suffer. Or did you? Were you completely unaware of how you humiliated me? How you ridiculed my every opinion until I had none? How you laughed at my taste, which I know is appalling but you didn't have to be so *cutting*. You didn't have to make fun so cruelly of me those few times I did open my mouth and voice a minor disagreement with something you said. I never, never in all the years of our marriage disagreed with anything important. Thank God Rupert was a boy and not a girl. You taught him such tosh, though. You were like a Nazi commandant, utterly unsympathetic, closed-minded, sexist and *stupid*. Yes, stupid, Henry. I used to think—you'd have me believe—that *I* was the idiot. I've discovered it was not me at all who was dumb, it was *you*. Horrid, cruel and nasty, nasty, nasty.' And she'd shake her head and tut-tut to herself and try to banish him from her thoughts but it was difficult. His malign presence often seemed to take over her entire mind and she had to ruthlessly exorcize him by chatting to someone, eating out, listening to music or talking books on her new Walkman.

She had the doctors in the hospital, the lawyers, draw up the relevant papers to give her complete control of business affairs. She had Henry declared legally incompetent, which seemed to everyone concerned the obvious thing to do. She already had a right to sign cheques, though she had never dared to take advantage of this facility as her husband

156

had queried every expenditure with MI5 thoroughness. So she had *carte blanche* to spend as she wished while in the process of taking over sole power of attorney.

'Sorry, Henry,' she told him in her mind, 'but you know what they say: "what you put out is what you get back".'

She, like Daniella and Marcello, went south. She said goodbye to Ariana and disappeared in a cab towards the airport, having purchased a new wardrobe of clothes on the Via Condotti. She had her hair newly styled, refusing, however, to be tamed. 'This is me,' she declared, 'and I'll not be toned down by the arbiters of so-called "good taste". I'm going to wear what I want from now on, see if I don't.'

She had fallen a bundle for Christian Lacroix rather than the elegant Armani, and favoured the more flamboyant boutiques rather than the stylish. Laden down with shiny designer carrier bags she had burst in on Ariana and Selina and announced that she had a taxi waiting outside to take her to the airport.

'Where are you going?' Ariana asked her, slightly bemused.

'Oh, I think Capri.' Gladys tossed her new sleek ruby-red bob and grinned at them. 'Capri sounds like my sort of place,' she told them, then embraced the two women abandonedly, kissing them on both cheeks in an excess of affection.

'Oh, thank you both,' she cried.

'Does Rupert know? That you're going off like that?' Ariana asked.

'I don't think so,' Gladys frowned.

'Don't you think you should tell him?' Ariana asked.

'I'm sure he's not interested in where I am,' Gladys replied. 'I'm sort of an embarrassment to him.' She shrugged. 'Anyhow, Selina here can tell him,' she added comfortably. 'And I wish you all the luck in the world, Selina. You've taken on quite a job, changing him.' And she hurried out and into her taxi.

'I hope she knows what she's doing,' Ariana remarked.

'I feel sure Gladys is fully in command of herself,' Selina laughed. 'She intends to make up for lost time and have a ball and I for one think she's got the right idea.'

'Come on, let's get a little squiffy,' Ariana said to Selina. 'Carlo is working late tonight and the children are tucked up in bed.'

They moved between the kitchen and the terrace while they drank a bottle of good wine between them and Ariana developed a superb sauce from peppers, onions and garlic, tomatoes, herbs for a pasta.

'You're happy with Carlo?' Selina asked tentatively after her second glass of wine. Ariana nodded.

'Yes. Oh, we've had our ups and downs.

Everyone does, but we've weathered them.'

'He ever given you a real problem?' Selina asked. Ariana squinted, her eyes watering as she chopped onions.

'There was a little secretary in FAO,' she told Selina. 'A pretty little thing called Gina. Greek, I think. All juvenile hero-worship, big adoring eyes. I know Carlo had a bit but it didn't last. I would have left him then but for the children.' She stared reflectively into the distance where the sun was setting, a fiery ball of molten gold over the dome of St Peter's. 'I'm glad I didn't,' she said, glancing at Selina. 'Experiences bind you together. The hum and hustle of life, the little things, irritations, small crises draw you together rather than the big things. He's like part of me. An essential part of our life together. Interwoven experiences. Sometimes I turn to him. Sometimes he turns to me. I'm used to him. He's my buddy, my friend.'

'That must be nice,' Selina said wistfully.

'Sex is only a small part of it. It's much more the growing together. The time spent with each other reaching decisions. The memories laced. No matter how hard you try they'll always be part of you.' She shook her head. 'I feel so sorry for Daniella and Rupert. There'll always be a bit of the one in the other's head and heart.'

'Maybe. But they were never *together*, Ariana, in the way you and Carlo are. I don't think Rupert ever *shared* anything of himself with anyone.'

'Except perhaps his father.'

'Even then it was one-sided. Much more the pupil-teacher relationship. It's not quite the same thing, is it?'

Ariana, who had been churning the dressing oils, the mustard, the vinegar together with the herbs and garlic, gave the servers to Selina to toss the salad.

'Now it's my turn,' she smiled. 'Are you in love with Rupert?'

'Good God no!'

'Then why on earth . . . ?'

'I know myself very well, Ariana. I'm selfish and quite terrifyingly self-sufficient. But I'd like a man in my life and Rupert fits the bill. As I've told you, I'll *develop* him. He's up for grabs. At the moment he's not sure if he's fish, fowl or good red herring and I'm here to . . .' she cast her eyes up to heaven, then said, ' . . . *mould* him.'

'Isn't that a bit like what he did to Daniella?' Ariana asked and Selina shrugged.

'So? A taste of his own medicine? Well, perhaps. But I'll teach him good ways. Open his mind. Don't worry,' she cried as she saw Ariana's expression, 'I know exactly what I'm doing. And I'll get him out of your hair as soon as he arrives.'

Selina was as good as her word. Rupert had barely stepped into his sister-in-law's hall, tired out after his travels, than he was whisked out into a bright yellow Fiat. Amid a lot of protests, waving and shouted farewells, the car took off on the wrong side of the road, a very alarmed Rupert in the passenger seat, and drove almost without stopping to Sorrento and the haven of a Grand Hotel.

CHAPTER TWENTY-THREE

Positano trips down in a long populated slope to the sea, brilliant blue streaked with light aquamarine. The slope is dotted with pink-roofed houses, little boutiques pressed into the hillside, fig and olive trees, vines and wisteria climbing everywhere. The view from the hotel high up above the little village was breathtaking and Daniella stretched and leaned over the balcony and drank in the shimmering sea crested with waves tipped with gold, the light dancing like fireflies over the radiant scene. She breathed in the scents, the hot smell of the warm sun and earth and the salt spray of the sea, the bouquet of perfumes from the abundant flowers, particularly the night-scented jasmine. She felt utterly relaxed, her body at peace, her nerves stilled, a huge warm glow at the centre of her being.

Then he said, emerging onto the balcony behind her, putting his arms around her, rubbing his cheek against her:

'I have to tell you something.'

Oh-oh, she thought, oh hell, oh damn, I knew it was too good to last. He's going to tell me something awful. He has a wife. He doesn't really love me.

Her peace of mind fled and she shivered, suddenly cold in the hot day, aware of what she had to lose, how fragile her happiness was.

'Don't, Marcello,' she pleaded. 'Don't tell me something that will spoil this. Please. I'd rather not know.'

He turned her around to face him.

'I have to,' he said.

Bella was here and Marcello knew there was no way he could brazen out an encounter with her and Daniella not guess. Positano was a very small place and the chances of them *not* bumping into each other were remote. Daniella was acutely sensitive to those around her, their feelings and their unspoken thoughts and he knew she would pick up immediately on the vibes there would always be between him and his mistress.

He had thought of leaving, throwing everything into the car, telling her he wanted to take her some other place, driving to Amalfi, but she'd know there was something behind his desire to leave. She was no fool and in any event he hated lies and deception and saw no real reason to dissimulate.

This place had special significance for her

and he knew she cherished their time together here and her laying of old ghosts. She would divine something was amiss if he tried to avoid his mistress or flee the place. He decided his best course, his only course, really, was to tell Daniella about Bella.

But he was scared. Daniella was such an innocent that he feared what her reaction would be and he knew he could not bear to lose her.

'Please don't spoil it,' she begged, looking at him with eyes huge with anxiety.

'I'll try not to, Dani. But I've got to be honest with you.'

'No. No. You haven't!' she cried.

But he ploughed on stubbornly. Now that it had been raised it would never lie down. It would be between them, she knew that. Marcello had to tell her for better or for worse.

'Listen. Remember that woman we saw last night in the piazza?'

'The beautiful voluptuous creature like someone out of a Visconti movie? Oh God,' her hand flew to her mouth, 'oh God, she's your wife!'

They had come into the square the previous night and Daniella had immediately remarked on the opulent charms of the woman sitting at a table, an elderly gentleman at her side. The fairy lights glimmered like a crown of stars around her and she had her head thrown back

163

and was laughing at something her companion was saying. Daniella had involuntarily plucked Marcello's sleeve and cried, 'Look at that beautiful woman, Marcello. How lovely she is,' and Marcello had taken her arm and suddenly turned and steered her away from the piazza towards the sea with some casual remark about the square being crowded.

'You are married to her. Oh God. I knew it was too good to be true.' She gazed at him now in panic and he could see the small pulse beating in her throat. He threw back his head and laughed.

'Oh no, no, no, Daniella, listen. I told you I was not married. I would not lie to you about something like that. No,' he became serious, 'but she was . . . my . . . er, mistress.' There, it was out. He dared not look at her. He frowned. 'It sounds so . . . for many years . . . I went . . .' he stumbled to a halt. Dear God, he prayed, let me not lose her. But the English, like the Americans, were such prudes. Who knew what she might expect of him? That he still be a virgin?

'You mean you went to her for sex?' Daniella forced him to look at her. Her eyes searched his and he longed to look elsewhere but could not. He had never felt so guilty in his life yet he knew he had no reason to be.

'Yes,' he said, tight-jawed. He was going to add that she gave him much more than sex, but decided not to. There were some things better

164

left unsaid. They stared at each other, he apprehensive, she wide-eyed, gazing at him.

'That's all right then,' she laughed. She touched his cheek. 'You meant it when you said you'd never told another woman you loved her?' He nodded, looking very relieved, took her hand and kissed the palm.

'Never,' he said.

'Well, I suppose you had to do something,' she shrugged.

'Come here,' he cried, suddenly pulling her into his arms. He was overcome with love for her, holding her close to him. 'Oh dearest girl, how I love you. You'll never know.'

And that was how Bella saw them as she looked upwards to the hotel. They stood there under the neon sign silhouetted against the moon on their balcony above the restaurant where she and the retired military man were dining. She felt the sharp sting of pain in her heart, then stifled it with unselfish determination and, lifting her glass of wine, turned to her companion, a brilliant and seductive smile on her face and proposed a toast to good health and happiness.

The cheque had been large. She would keep it. She had not promised results. She had no qualms about that. It would serve the old woman right. Interfering old witch. Bella knew precisely what had gone on in the powerful old lady's mind that day. Break it up because Daniella was married! Because she would be a divorcée! Did she take Bella for a complete fool? Yes, and if Daniella, that lovely clear-eyed girl she had seen with Marcello the evening before, the girl he had so tenderly, protectively shielded from her, his mistress, if Daniella had never been married, was a good Catholic virgin and had never had to get a divorce, Katerina Vestori would still, Bella was certain, have sent for her and asked her to break it up. No, those reasons were facile, mere excuses.

What she wanted, Katerina Vestori, was full possession of her son, except in the area of his sexual needs and that, the old lady implied, Bella could deal with. She had been very content with Marcello living at home at her beck and call, her companion, her devoted son and employee and she wanted it to stay that way. Bella ministering to his carnal requirements when he came to Rome on his weekly visits. Katerina had it exactly the way she wanted.

The trouble was, so did Bella. She too was perfectly happy with the arrangement. It would be unbearably painful to give him up. She too did not want change.

Bella understood herself and realised that she would never really get over Marcello. She loved him, was in love with him as much as she was capable of loving any man and that was why she was unselfish enough to let him go, set him free.

She'd lost him anyway. If she broke the romance up—and, knowing how loyal and faithful Marcello was she doubted very much that she could succeed—she would lose him. He had obstinately clung to her all these years in spite of her efforts to set him on the right path. He was a one-woman man and once he fell in love there would be no going back. And if she did manage to break it up Marcello would hate her. She knew him well enough to be certain of that. Katerina Vestori had not thought it through to the end. She had simply wanted to have things go on as they were, unable or unwilling to understand that things *never* went on the same. Change was inevitable in this life and no one, not even Katerina, could turn the clock back.

Bella smiled to herself. Why be up-front with the old autocrat? Take the money, warn Marcello and report she'd failed. What could the old bag do?

CHAPTER TWENTY-FOUR

The sky was 'thick with patines of bright gold', stars bright as silver dollars winking and blinking on the heavy blue velvet backdrop.

'Isn't that your ex?' Daniella asked as they sat in the brightly lit piazza drinking *strega*, and eating a delicious tagliolini.

Bella had arrived in the little square, made an entrance like a diva or pop star, Daniella thought apprehensively, alarmingly glamorous on the arm of her elderly gallant. She moved confidently, sure of the reception she would receive, of the admiring stares, the male smacking of lips.

Marcello nodded. 'Yes,' he said. 'That's Bella.'

He glanced nervously at Daniella's face but it revealed little of what she felt. She was used to hiding her feelings and she smiled blandly at him, trying not to show her insecurity, her lack of confidence. She knew that if she was too clinging, too needy, Marcello might be disconcerted, might become irritated, and she was acutely aware that she must not make the same mistake twice. She was not going to become a victim once more.

She knew that there was something intrinsically off-putting about over-dependence. She had to stop herself from constantly asking him, 'Do you really love me? How can you have had someone like her in your life but choose me instead? Are you sure you really, really love me? Are you sure?' Letting her need for him, her need for reassurance show. I have to trust him, she told herself, show him I believe him. She needed to be his partner, his equal. So she did not allow him to see how that beautiful, composed, sophisticated woman disconcerted her.

It was difficult but she managed. To their surprise Bella moved across the square in a beeline towards them. She wore a white silk flowing dress-coat split up the sides and bordered with gold thread, Cretan design, and under it slim silk Egyptian trousers and a gold-bordered chemise. The fine material of the coat floated out about her body as she sailed past the crowded tables like a beautiful, gossamar white moth, the fairy lights catching the glint of gold embroidery and the jewels around her throat and in her ears. How could he prefer little mousy me to this goddess? Daniella asked herself in awed admiration.

'Marcello, how good to see you,' she greeted him effusively when she reached him and turned to Daniella. 'And you must be Daniella. How pretty you are! The good things I heard about you do not do you justice.'

Who? From whom? What had she heard? The questions buzzed around Daniella's head. Bella gave them no chance to reply but turned to her companion who had just caught up with her and puffing and blowing stood beside her mopping his brow.

'Generalissimo Raphael Donizetti. This is Marcello Vestori, an old friend of mine, and this delightful girl is Daniella Weston. Am I right?' She smiled radiantly at them both. 'May we join you, just for a moment? We are booked for dinner at Antonio's and we are on our way there. But when I see you here, my old

169

friend, I naturally come over to bid you good evening.'

She sat at the table beside them and waving at a waiter ordered a bottle of San Pellegrino.

'I'll have a glass. The walk from the hotel was,' she waved her hand in an incredibly langorous gesture, 'exhausting!'

'What do you mean, the good things you heard?' Marcello asked. There was more here than met the eye. No one knew about Daniella, so it didn't make sense. 'Where did you hear these things?'

'At your mother's home in Florence.'

Bella was tranquil and seemed unperturbed, but Marcello gasped and spluttered. 'Mamma? Is she spying on me?' he cried. Bella nodded.

'Probably,' she smiled. 'She is frightened, Marcello. She does not want to lose you. Don't agitate yourself. Your Mamma has forgotten that you have grown up. That you are a big boy now.' Her eyes danced and Daniella felt a moment of anger at the woman's self-confidence.

Marcello gaped at her. 'Mamma interfering? *Oh Jesu Christo*!'

'Don't be afraid, Marcello . . .'

'I'm not afraid. I'm angry!' Marcello protested.

'Well, don't be,' Bella smiled. 'Listen, she's an old woman. She's frightened. Simply keep out of her way. For a while. And Daniella, hurry a divorce through. Go to Las Vegas if you have to. Or Scotland. I believe they are very sympathetic in those places. Anyhow, rush it through and then marry each other quietly somewhere. You can always make your vows again in church, later on when the fuss dies down. But Marcello, keep out of your mother's way.'

'She asked you to come here? She wanted you to cause harm? To Daniella?' The thought filled him with fury.

Bella nodded. 'Yes. She wanted me to break it up. But you must not hate her. As I said, she is possessive.'

'No, she has gone too far. She really has.'

'Fuss?' Daniella was murmuring. She had not considered Marcello's family, or even given a thought to the fact that he had one. Now, it appeared he not only had a mistress but a formidable Mamma. She shivered and slipped her hand into Marcello's. I will not allow this to upset me, she thought. Bella was on her side. That much was obvious.

'Take her to England, Marcello. Open a Vestori's store in Beauchamp Place or Sloane Street. Your mother has asked you often enough to branch out. Your brother-in-law will be delighted. He'll co-operate. Well, do it!'

Marcello looked at her gratefully. 'As usual you are wise, Bella,' he told her. 'Yes, it is a perfect plan.' Then he laughed. 'Well, maybe not perfect, but manageable.'

His Mamma was on the warpath. He knew

the signs well. Well, he'd avoid her. He'd move up the coast, relax for a while, spend time in his beloved's arms, then go to London. He would fax his brother-in-law Christano in Florence and tell him he was moving there for a while with a view to opening a new store. Christano would be delighted to have his charming brother-in-law out of the way. He'd meet Daniella's parents, start the ball rolling on the divorce proceedings.

He covered Bella's hand with his. 'Thank you,' he said softly, and she knew their relationship was at an end.

When she rose she smiled at him and he saw her eyes were shimmering with unshed tears.

Then she floated away from them, her silken robe billowing out behind her, the little Generalissimo running to keep up with her.

CHAPTER TWENTY-FIVE

Rupert had completely changed character and to his surprise he was utterly enamoured of his new role. He found it much easier and more comfortable not to have to be right all the time. It was quite pleasant not to be absolutely sure about things, to be occasionally wrong. Not to have the final word, not to have to make *all* the decisions. The part of 'head of the household' had not really suited him, he decided. It had been tailor-made for his father, but not for him.

He did not blame his father for moulding him in his likeness. His father had thought he was doing the right thing. And Rupert still looked up to his father. That powerful influence in his life could not so easily be shrugged off.

Rupert decided that if he ever had children he would encourage them to treat every human being as an equal.

He confided this to Selina in bed in Sorrento as she slid away from him over to her side of the bed after they had made love. They had 'his side' and 'her side' by now, preferred and respected. Territorial except when they melted into each other's arms.

Selina was an education; in every department she kept surprising him. When he made love to Daniella he expected, no, demanded, that she be a quiet, malleable partner. Selina had, he thought, radical notions about lovemaking, turning all his preconceived ideas upside down, and he, being in no state to insist on his tried and true method, allowed her to bully him, take the initiative and have her way with him. Again, he found it exciting, provocative and much more stimulating than the old in and out he'd been in the habit of with his wife.

That was when he'd told her about his decision. Amazed at what had just happened between them in bed he'd thought of his father's instructions as to sexual congress and said:

'If I ever have children I'll tell them to treat all human beings as equal. No authority figures.'

'You'll have the little sprogs running about like tinkers,' Selina laughed. 'Undisciplined. Wild. Too far the other way. Ah well, it's your choice.' Then peering at him through her thick lashes she added, 'But if you've elected me as mum you're on the wrong track entirely.'

He blushed. 'I thought, in a little while you might marry me, and then, eventually we'd have children. If I'm able. Daniella says the doctor said . . .'

Selina leaned on her elbow and stared at him. 'Don't worry about that,' she told him kindly. 'We can go into that later. But Rupe, why on earth do you want to marry me? I've treated you abominably.'

'I don't think so. Your love has been tough. That's okay. I was impossible, I see that now. I like the way you treat me. Order me about. And I don't like being single.'

'Without a slave!'

'No. I won't let you give me motives that simply are not fact. No, Selina, without a *companion*. Not without a slave. I want, no, need you to be a permanent part of my life and I'm not ashamed of that need.'

He was gripping his arms behind his head

174

and looking at her earnestly. 'Oh, I know I initially missed Daniella doing the household duties, all the things I had become used to, that my father said were women's duties. Only none of that seems to matter any more. I could always get a woman in to do those things . . .'

'Or a man . . .' she amended.

He glanced at her. 'What?' Then as her meaning became clear, 'Oh yes. Or a man,' he laughed. 'But I miss companionship. Not that I had any with Daniella . . . but this time with you. I'm going to miss your company dreadfully when we go back.'

He took a sharp breath as he felt her hand roving around a strategically sensitive part of his anatomy.

'Is that all you'll miss?' She was laughing as she slid a long honey-coloured leg over his thighs and wriggled onto him, kissing his lips with tiny little stabbing pecks. 'Not this, or this, or this, or this?' He let out a long moan and taking his arms from behind his head he wrapped them around her, pressing her close.

'Oh yes, yes, yes, yes, yes,' he cried. 'What do you think?'

But she decided it was worth it. If the eventuality was pain and heartache, then so be it. If he reverted to type (although she thought it unlikely; his conversion seemed complete, based on enlightenment, not infatuation) then she'd deal with that in the fullness of time. Live now, pay later. But at the moment she was something she'd never been before in the whole of her angst-ridden, pushy, ambition-motivated life: content, at peace with the world, dare she say it, happy.

*   *   *

They had been in Sorrento a week when they heard about Gladys.

One evening at dinner in the hotel a thin, overdone-on-the-tan, stylishly-dressed couple approached them, striding haughtily through the room, glancing down their noses at the other diners as they passed.

'We are the Wilmington-Smythes,' they announced in unison when they reached the table where Rupert and Selina sat. 'We're English,' they said as if that explained everything.

The man was tall, his cavernous face leathery, sun-scorched, his silver hair combed immaculately over his bare scalp, wearing a dapper cream woven silk suit and a striped pink shirt, pale mauve tie in a perfect Windsor knot, and the vee of a mauve silk handkerchief hanging tastefully over the breast pocket. 'Will you join us for coffee on the terrace? We would be honoured,' he asked.

Rupert could see the wicked glint in Selina's eyes and his first instinct was to refuse politely. In the old days he would have announced firmly, 'No, thank you', but he deferred to

Selina who said, 'How very kind. We'd love to.'

The woman wore a neat little green silk shantung dress, too short for a woman of her age and her hair, flat against her head, made her look like an ageing Modigliani. It was dyed golden blond, harsh on her face and tarnished by the sun. 'You're the only other English here,' she said, looking around the dining room disdainfully as if the other occupants were beneath contempt.

'And that makes us kosher, does it?' Selina asked in an amused voice, but the Wilmington Smythes took her seriously.

'Of course,' the woman said complacently.

'Are you of the Jewish faith?' the man asked suspiciously.

Afterwards Selina told Rupert that she nearly said yes. Just to see their reaction. 'Bet they'd have dropped us like hot bricks.' But she didn't, preferring to, as she said, 'Allow them to entertain us for an hour.'

And they did. They implied retirement from vast enterprises, though what enterprises Selina and Rupert never found out in spite of probing enquiries. They name-dropped relentlessly, talking about Roger and the Weinbergs, Taki and Elton. Ships: the Goslings, Shoes, the Vestoris, and ceiling-wax, the great Carboni (Princess Carboni was mentioned frequently by the pet name of Ca-Ca) candle-manufacturing firm, cabbages; a world-famous megastore owner who had been knighted, and of course the kings of Greece, Spain and other European monarchies, including the Grimaldis.

Then suddenly, to their amazement, Gladys's name popped up.

' ... and our dear friend Gladys Weston. Name same as yours.'

'Yes, she's my mother.'

This statement, made in all innocence by Rupert, caused obvious admiration and respect. A flurry of excitement shivered through the Wilmington-Smythes.

'Gosh! It's a small world, isn't it?' Hero-worship brimmed in two unblinking pairs of eyes and chairs moved a little nearer, voices a little more confiding, less cautious.

'She's such a good friend of the King of Greece,' murmured the woman, whose first name turned out to be Phillida ('Call me Philly. And this is Bernard. His friends,' with a coy smile, 'call him Bunny.').

Selina said, 'Your mum must be moving in very high circles indeed.'

'My mum?' Rupert exclaimed in disbelief.

'How cute,' Philly twinkled.

'What?'

'Calling her "my mum".'

'Well, she is!' Rupert said looking a little bemused.

'Where did you say you met her?' Selina shot him a warning glance.

'I told you. The Duke's yacht in Golf Juan.

Near Cannes. They'd sailed from Capri. We left the boat there and came to Naples.'

'She's a real swinger,' Bunny grinned, 'your mum.' He almost winked. It would become a standard joke. The Weston boy who called his mater 'mum'.

'I hope you don't take offence but I did feel her companion was just a teeny bit ... youthful,' Philly said carefully, pursing her lips in disapproval.

'Umm,' Bunny agreed, sipping his espresso. 'Just a tad.'

'Oh? Who is it now? She goes through men like they might become extinct,' Selina remarked, eyes wicked, and Rupert choked on his coffee.

The Wilmington-Smythe eyes blinked rapidly but, used to the idiosyncrasies of the rich and famous, they took it in their stride.

'The Conte Massey de la Croche is a *very* young man,' Philly told them. 'Descendent of kings, I'm told. In his early thirties. A playboy. Very good looking.'

'Sounds good to me,' Selina remarked complacently.

'He's got no money though,' Bunny informed them.

'Mother has,' Rupert said. He'd discovered the situation *vis-à-vis* his parents' finances through the family lawyer and some papers that had been sent to him to sign which had taken his breath away.

179

'Ah!' Bunny exclaimed knowingly, then glancing at Philly he rose. 'Well, it's been very nice chatting with you,' he said. 'But we must retire.'

'Hit the hay,' Philly rose too, holding out her hand.

'We have an early start.' Bunny shook their hands in a stiff formal pump-action. 'Off to the Contessa's in Napoli.' He used the Italian pronunciation.

'It's all go, go, go, isn't it?' Selina laughed, but the Wilmington-Smythes did not hear the irony in her voice.

They shook hands all round, bidding farewell to each other and exchanging promises to meet in the future that neither party intended to keep.

'We're not important enough,' Selina said when they'd gone. 'Poor people.'

'Oh, I don't know. They seem happy enough to me, doing what they like doing.'

Selina looked at him, her face suddenly serious.

'How very mature of you, Rupert. You really have changed.' She smiled at him tenderly in the shadowy gloom of the terrace.

The lights were circling the mountains and hills like glittering necklaces. A huge pink moon the colour of candy-floss hung low over the bay which was a depthless navy-blue.

'Yes, well,' Rupert smiled at her. 'Fancy my mother. Off with a gigolo!'

'You're not appalled, Rupe?'

He shook his head. 'No. I can see why. She's been kept down for so long. She's having fun at last.'

'And you don't mind?'

'No. No, Selina, I don't anymore. I'm not jealous. You see, I'm having fun too.'

'And your father? Do you worry about him like you used to?'

'Not any more. He's in good hands. There's nothing more can be done for him.' He glanced at her, loving the clear, slim lines of her body, the confident tilt of her chin.

'I hope you'll ... stay with me, Selina. I think I might lose it again without you. I know I've nothing much to offer you but ...'

'You have, Rupe. If only you knew! You have.' She sounded serious, sincere, and his heart lifted.

'I want commitment,' he said, suddenly aware nothing else would do.

'Okay. You're on,' she said lightly, rising, gathering her cashmere wrap around her.

'What?' He was confused by her precipitation.

'I said, you silly boy, yes. As soon as you get your divorce, yes.' And she threw the wrap over her shoulders like a toreador and strode into the restaurant and away.

He stared after her as she wove confidently through the almost deserted room. He could not believe his luck.

She'd agreed. She'd said yes. He made a fist and punched the air above him. He mouthed 'yes' silently.

He thought of his mother. He was no longer angry with her. He could understand her now, how she felt, what motivated her. He smiled to himself, stretched his arms above his head, rose and followed Selina to bed.

EPILOGUE

The funeral service in the hospital was short. Rupert had been uncertain what to do as Henry had not believed in anything even remotely spiritual. He had often derided what he collectively called mumbo-jumbo, meaning all orthodox religion, any form of meditation, any search for truth. Even the Green parties were, in his closed-minded opinion, tarred with the same brush and deserving only of contempt.

So it was with difficulty that Rupert, not wishing to insult his father's narrow-minded ideas, if such negative opinions could be so termed, tried to solve the problem of what kind of service should be held. It was Selina who solved the problem for him.

'Do it for yourself, Rupert. After all, if your father's right he'll know nothing about it. And if he's wrong then he's in the middle of the biggest shock and therefore otherwise preoccupied.'

So Rupert eventually hedged his bets by having a simple Presbyterian ceremony in Twilight House where Henry had spent his last days, and another more formal service in Golders Green where he was to be cremated.

The chapel ceremony was sparsely attended. Except for the family there were few people there. It appeared Henry Weston had no friends.

Rupert was not surprised. He remembered how isolated he and Daniella had been when they were married. They had been terribly alone in the house in Lansdowne Road. His father's derisive precepts did not make one lovable or popular and his beliefs that everyone was after something did not help to make friends.

Rupert had assumed he would be the chief mourner but at the last moment at Twilight House, when the clergyman had already begun and everyone was singing 'Abide With Me', Gladys had erupted into the chapel and, weeping copiously, hurried up the aisle to stand beside her son. Trailing after her was a tall, handsome, olive-skinned young man who obviously worked out and was, as Bunny Wilmington-Smythe had described, 'a tad young for her'. He looked, however, very good-humoured and, Selina said afterwards, not too bright.

'I wouldn't say he was loaded with brains,' she commented, 'as he obviously is with muscle. Which no doubt is exactly what your mother wants.'

Rupert was, it must be confessed, a little put-out by his mother's sudden appearance. He had, since their return to London, visited his father regularly on Sundays. What this accomplished, or whether it accomplished anything, he did not know. His father sat or lay motionless in his wheelchair or his bed like an effigy, seemingly mentally somewhere else. But Rupert felt better after his visits.

'You're doing your duty,' Selina said, 'and that makes you feel good.'

Selina sometimes came with him and just recently, until his father's second fatal stroke, they'd brought the baby with them.

He and Selina had had their ups and downs during the intervening years, neither of them adapting easily to the dual state. But they both worked hard at it, were prepared to discuss their differences and stuck to the rule of never going to sleep on an argument or quarrel. This led inevitably to many late-night discussions but it worked.

Rupert went to the doctor, dealt in a mature fashion with his low sperm count and Selina got pregnant.

When this happened Selina was at first bewildered. Always in charge of herself she was initially dismayed at the changes in her body but to her surprise and Rupert's delight she adapted quite spectacularly to the whole concept and became to her own astonishment a devoted and doting mother.

When they brought little Jonathan in to see Henry, Rupert's father did not show any more emotion than his usual spaced-out indifference to the world in general. But it pleased Rupert. His heart swelled with joy when, visiting his sick father, he looked across and saw Selina, her face soft with love, cooing at her child, their son wrapped in his comforter, undaunted as yet by social niceties, burping, cooing, his little fists waving aimlessly about. Rupert's heart nearly burst with pride and joy and he hoped then that Selina, when her gaze met his, could see into his heart, for he was still unable to express the magnitude of that tumultuous feeling.

So Rupert was a bit disgruntled when his mother appeared and upstaged him and Henry, focusing all attention on herself. Especially, Rupert told himself, when the deceased had not had so much as a postcard since she'd disappeared five years ago. When she'd dumped him.

Since then, like Ulysses, she had sailed around the Greek seas, partying, her young Adonis in attendance, keeping her entertained. Singing, as Selina said, for his supper. Word had floated back to them, first from further afield, Acapulco and Palm Beach, then Turkey, Sardinia and finally the Greek islands. Moonlit romps, sundowners, hectic parties, all mentioned casually *en passant*. Rupert decided his mother must have been another character altogether than the woman he had known all his life.

* * *

It seemed, Rupert had remarked to Selina, as if in her greedy pursuit of pleasure she was plundering the world.

Another surprise lay in store for Rupert that grey London day. The clouds, like chiffon scarves, saffron-coloured from the reflected glow of the city, streaked the sky and lay low over the buildings. Every now and then they wept, slow acid tears.

The mourners piled into limos outside the church and the coffin processed in undignified haste through traffic jams to the crematorium.

In Golders Green, however, Daniella, Marcello and the whole Vestori family waited dressed in sombre if stylish black. Rupert was touched. He nodded to his ex-wife who seemed another person to him as she stood there, beautiful, smart, calmly confident, holding her husband's hand.

An official had arrived out of the little chapel to receive the coffin. He was whispering sibilantly that they were late and he had another cremation in half an hour so they must get a move on. Gladys held out her arm and Rupert entered the chapel with his mother leaning heavily on it, the attendant urging them forward and the Vestoris falling in behind.

'Here we all are,' Daniella whispered to her sister who sat beside her, flanked by her two children. 'All together. Can you believe it?'

Ariana was over in London on a visit. She

hugged Daniella.

'The shop is doing well, I hear?' she asked rhetorically, smiling at Daniella who squeezed her hand.

'Absolutely. It's done brilliantly. Marcello is the golden-haired boy now.'

'And his Mamma? Has Katerina come around yet?'

Marcello smiled and put his arm around his wife. 'Sure. Of course. I always knew she would.'

Daniella winked at her sister. Katerina Vestori would never fully accept her daughter-in-law, but she was careful not to allow Marcello to see this. Every time she was cruel or slighting to Daniella behind his back her daughter-in-law made an excuse and left and Marcello, hating to be apart from her for a moment would follow. Katerina soon got the message. Over the years she had learned to watch her manners if she wanted to see her son, and the old lady had to concede a grudging victory to Daniella.

And Daniella was grateful to her mother-in-law who had, if only she knew, given her a confidence she had never before possessed. She had been Daniella's first opponent and first victory. Katerina provided the affirmation Daniella needed that she had become a whole, strong person.

The coffin made its stately way through the curtain into the fiery furnace. The cleric muttered on about dust and to the relief of the living it finally disappeared. Gladys abruptly stopped crying, raised her veil and kissed Rupert. Then, catching sight of his expression, said:

'Well, I was married to him for thirty years. I've been paying for Twilight House. It's only right I say goodbye. Which I'm enjoying, Rupert, I have to say.' Seeing Selina she cried, 'Ah! So this is the baby.'

'Your grands—'

'*Don't say that word!*' Gladys commanded. Glancing at the child she cooed mechanically for a second or two, then taking her handsome lover's arm waved a little to the right and left as if, Selina whispered, she was the Queen Mum, and disappeared the wrong way out, into the crowd for the next cremation who were queuing up waiting to enter. The attendant hissed loudly, '*Not* that way, madam. Please not that way.' Gladys paid no attention and proceeded on her merry way.

She had not recognised her ex-daughter-in-law and Daniella stared after as she left causing chaos in her wake.

'Who would have thought,' she mused.

'Indeed,' Ariana said. 'Or about you for that matter.'

'Me?'

'Yes, you, Miss Innocent. I never thought you had it in you.'

'You mean Katerina? No, I surprised

189

myself. She's ready to behave herself now so Marcello and I are going to move to Italy. To Rome. I'll be happier there. No sad memories.'

Ariana was gathering up the children, watching Selina and Rupert leave by the correct side door. She nodded towards them.

'They look so content, don't you think?'

'Umm. Selina is obviously enjoying motherhood.' Daniella glanced at her sister. 'As no doubt I will. In seven months' time.'

Ariana let out a squeal, then hid her face as she heard the outraged hiss and saw the shocked faces of the next crowd entering the chapel with their coffin. She hurried the children into the grey day. Outside she hugged her sister. 'Oh, I'm so glad. Congratulations!' Then, holding her a little away, 'No, Daniella. I did not mean Signora Vestori when I said I thought you never had it in you.'

'Oh? Then who did you mean?'

'I meant you and Rupert. I thought you'd stay locked into that misery for the rest of your life.'

Daniella smiled and the happiness lit up her face like a sunrise.

Rupert whispered something to Selina, who nodded and, tenderly shielding her baby, began walking to the cars. He came over and stood in front of Daniella.

'Hello, Rupert. How are you?' she said. 'I can tell you're happy. I can see it in your face.'

'And so are you,' he said. 'I too can see it in you.'

She smiled at him and nodded. She didn't need to say anything. Ariana moved away over to the cars. It began to rain.

'Do you remember that day? In Lansdowne Road? You left me. You walked out. I watched in speechless bewilderment. I couldn't believe it.'

She nodded. 'I remember. It was the beginning of everything right for us.' She pressed the button and her umbrella shot up, framing her face.

'I never thought I'd hear myself say this but I'm glad you did, Daniella. Very glad and grateful.' He frowned, then added, 'Did you plan it?' he asked.

'No,' she said. 'It was a spur of the moment decision.'

The rain had suddenly grown heavier, beating a sharp tattoo on her umbrella, sheeting down. People began hurrying for shelter. Selina slammed the car door to prevent the baby getting wet. Ariana's voice floated back to Daniella, caught on the wind. Rupert and Daniella stood facing each other. 'Goodbye, Rupert,' she told him.

'Goodbye, Dani,' he said, smiling at her. 'I'm sorry for the pain I caused you.'

'I know that,' she replied.

Daniella, glancing over her shoulder, could see Marcello beckoning her, 'Hurry, your feet will get wet,' holding the car door open for her. Selina was staring out of the other car, her face blurred by the thick curtain of rain spattering her window.

Daniella looked back at Rupert. 'Be happy, Rupert,' she told him, and added, 'You know that spur of the moment decision?' He nodded. 'Well, I think it was the best decision I ever made in my life. For both of us.' Then she hurried over to the cars where her love was waiting.